WEEKEND ROMANCE

WEEKEND ROMANCE

•

WILMA FASANO

AVALON BOOKS
NEW YORK

PRINTED IN THE UNITED STATES OF AMERICA
ON ACID-FREE PAPER
BY HADDON CRAFTSMEN, BLOOMSBURG, PENNSYLVANIA

To Wendy Corsi Staub
Cupid Literary Services
Thank you for your advice and encouragement

Chapter One

The spiffy strawberry-red Neon shuddered as Lisa Bannerman turned off the highway and into a driveway bordered by bulldozed stumps with dirt clinging to the roots. Lisa shuddered in sympathy.

This had to be the place. Gritting her teeth, she eased the car through the mud, trying to avoid the deepest ruts. So maybe Pink Sally, as Lisa had affectionately named the car, wasn't a Mercedes or a BMW, but it was new and it was hers—or would be if the bank didn't repossess it.

At the end of the long driveway, a rusty brown station wagon sat alone on an unpaved parking lot. A new cement-block building squatted ominously behind it. A sign on a post read, *The Lunenburg Whaler, Chester, Nova Scotia. For bookings, call, or inquire within.* A phone number followed.

This didn't look much like the brochure Lisa had received after she'd inquired about the job. It didn't look

1

much like an inn in need of a social and recreation director.

She parked the car and hesitated a moment before she got out. The emerald lawn of the brochure was in reality a mixture of dirt and gravel. Instead of sweeping steps leading to a welcoming front porch, a grungy sheet of plywood slanted up to the front door. Over everything hung the smell of wet cement.

Lisa hesitated, then shrugged. Student loans and car payments didn't go away.

The makeshift ramp bounced beneath her feet with every step. She grasped the door handle and tugged open the heavy front door.

The lobby matched the outside. Lisa squinted in the dim light provided by a single low-wattage bulb. She paused.

An old gray filing cabinet and a battered desk loomed across the room from her. An open newspaper and the soles of shoes occupied the top of the desk. The newspaper was attached to hands, and the soles, belonging to flip-flop sandals, dangled at the end of long furry legs which were crossed at the ankles. The fur ended with khaki shorts.

What had she gotten herself into? For a moment she was grateful the person behind the newspaper ignored her. Once she stopped walking, total silence stalked her—no comforting sound of saws and hammers, no cheerful chatter of workmen.

She was alone with whoever lurked above the hairy legs.

The owner of the flip-flops observed Lisa over the top of his newspaper as she blinked in the dim light. He'd had a fleeting impression of a curvaceous figure and luscious legs topped by windblown dark hair and soft brown eyes.

Unless he was mistaken, right now, she also had an attitude. If so, he couldn't really blame her.

He reproached himself for letting her come here. He was an efficient businessman, a troubleshooter, the person whom management sent out to take over unprofitable inns, or, as in this case, to get new ones up and running; he didn't need laid-off high-school English teachers on his team.

Somehow when he'd heard her voice on the phone, smooth as warm honey, he'd been unable to resist her. Instead of admitting it was no use, he'd found himself saying yes, she could send a résumé, yes, she could come for an interview. Yes, he'd send out a brochure describing the inn.

After he'd hung up and it was too late, he'd regained his sanity.

This woman wasn't qualified to be a social and recreation director. He'd advertised that position because Jennifer, owner of the company, had expected it, but common sense told him he didn't need anyone to direct recreation for a good while yet.

Jennifer was grooming him to become one of the four people at the top. He admired her business acumen, and he needed her goodwill.

The big challenge—how could he let Ms. Curvaceous down easy? If she had any concern for appearances—his or the inn's—she'd run a mile, for sure.

He grimaced as he thought of how he looked this morning. The truth was he'd forgotten she was coming. He'd had every intention of meeting her in a dark suit, a white shirt, and a tie. He'd had every intention of being businesslike and intimidating when he explained to her that, no, the organization didn't really have a job for her.

She stood in front of him, screwing up her eyes as if she hoped this whole scene, and him with it, would go away.

Should he be rude? Would that cause her to leave on her own? Maybe not. She was, he knew from her résumé, twenty-six, only three years younger than himself. She might well have stubborn staying power.

He'd play it by ear. Somehow, some way, he'd have to say no, gently or otherwise. In today's business climate, success wasn't built on giving people jobs because they fancied they wanted them.

Lisa shifted from one foot to the other. She couldn't stand here all day. Unpalatable though the idea was, she'd have to get the attention of Hairy Legs.

"Hmm," she said, peering at the headline on her side of the paper. "Fishermen unhappy with the government again?"

Hairy Legs grunted and turned the page. His hands were strong and brown and masculine. From habit, Lisa looked for a ring and found none. Not that it mattered.

Right now, she didn't have the time or inclination to become interested in any man. She had to meet her car payments, work on her student loans, earn enough money to get her own apartment. Living at home didn't sit well after seven and a half years of independence.

She looked again at the man in front of her. He seemed a dreadful boor—probably just the caretaker, but still . . .

She cleared her throat discreetly. "It's really quite a nice day out. Much brighter than in here."

Silence.

All right. She squared her shoulders and pretended that her fuchsia suit was of the softest suede, and that her shiny black shoes were of supple Italian leather. She cleared her throat again, loudly this time, and drew herself up to her full five foot six. "I am Elizabeth Louise Bannerman." She added, more graciously, "My friends call me Lisa. I'd like to see the manager."

The paper didn't move, but a voice behind it, a deep, masculine, and not completely unpleasant voice asked, "What can I do for you, Elizabeth Louise?"

"I would like to see the manager."

The paper dropped. "I'm the manager."

Oh! Handsome enough, she supposed, if you liked the sort of looks that belonged to the wolf in "Little Red Riding Hood." The man wore an old brown tank top, spattered with paint, over the khaki shorts. His bare arms were as hairy and as muscle-bound as his legs.

Reddish-brown hair, almost a mahogany hue, covered his head. He watched Lisa with light hazel eyes, wolf's eyes. Dark mahogany eyebrows, turned up at the ends, added to the wolfish appearance, as did white teeth in a lean, tanned face.

The better to eat you with, my dear.

She shook off her qualms and determined to get the job. Although whatever this heap of dirt, concrete, and sheetrock would do with a social director, she couldn't imagine.

That wasn't her problem.

High-school English teachers laid off in their second year because of cutbacks couldn't afford to be fussy.

"Hello. I'm Lisa Bannerman," she repeated, "and I'm here to be interviewed for the job of social director."

"Oh, hi, Lisa," Hairy Legs said cheerfully enough. He swung his feet off the desk. The chair legs bounced on the plywood floor, sending up gossamer puffs of dust.

When he stood, he towered over her by a good six inches. "Have a seat," he said.

She looked around.

"Oh, oh, yes, of course. Here." He stood up and handed his plain wooden chair across the desk. "Take mine."

She laid her purse and folder of materials on the dusty

desk, then took the proffered chair in both hands. Her hand grazed one of his, disturbing her more than such a casual contact should.

She looked up and smiled to distract his attention, then gingerly placed the chair on the floor a decorous three feet in front of the desk. She retrieved her belongings and sat down primly, crossing her legs at the ankles and pulling her skirt over her knees.

"Uh—" Hairy Legs leaned over the desk. He put out his hand. "I'm Clinton Daniels, managing this inn for Jennifer and Silas Masters, owners of the S and J chain of country inns."

If she stood, the purse, folder, and everything else would slide onto the floor. She'd already hesitated too long for good manners, so she put out her hand to meet his, taking a deep breath to ward off unwelcome sensations.

He had a nice handshake—warm and firm. When he held her hand a moment too long, it tingled all the way up to the elbow. His wolfish smile assured her he knew that.

He perched on the desk and leaned forward as if he wished to intimidate her. The very idea! He'd find *that* would take more than bulging muscles and an in-her-face manner!

Whenever he flexed his dangling foot, the heel of the sandal hit the sole with a steady rhythmic slap, slap, slap. He had interesting feet too, strong and brown and masculine, just like his hands.

Lisa reminded herself firmly that she was here to get a job, not to check out the manager, especially such a rude, boorish, impossible manager.

Clinton Daniels scrutinized the young woman sitting before him. Her chocolate-brown eyes twinkled as if she continuously suppressed laughter. Feathery bangs ruffled across her forehead. The rest of her hair was cut like a boy's, the short unruly curls looking as if they'd been swept by a strong wind. Her peaches-and-cream complexion had just a smattering of freckles above a straight nose. Her cheekbones were classic, and he'd gotten a glance of dimpled knees. Her bright pink suit was enchanting.

The total package resembled the irresistible voice on the telephone. Telling her to get lost would not be easy.

She didn't resemble any of the other candidates. They'd been cool and poised and confident. They all reminded him of Jennifer.

Lisa would brighten up the place. No doubt about that. With the pink suit, she wore shiny black earrings and shiny black pumps with heels like stilts, and she carried a shiny black purse. She smelled like garden flowers.

He had to get this inn up and running, so he could turn it over to another manager. Then he could leave the rural scene behind him and head back to Toronto. He couldn't afford to be sidetracked by enthusiasm and dimpled knees.

"So," he said, "you're here for a job interview, are you?"

"Yes," Lisa said. "For the position of social director."

Clinton stared at her without speaking and continued to thump the heel of his dangling sandal against his foot.

She had to say something. The silence scraped her nerves like fingernails on a blackboard.

"I believe you have a copy of my résumé." She made a valiant effort to establish eye contact.

He waved vaguely in the direction of the battered filing cabinet. "I think it's in there somewhere, along with twenty or thirty others."

"Oh."

Twenty or thirty others for this job too? She thought of next month's car payment. She'd have to try harder.

"I've an extra copy here if you'd like." She inhaled and began to blow the dust off her folder, then stopped abruptly, opened it, and paused. Her thumb and forefinger held the crisp white corner of a résumé.

"No, no, don't bother. I don't care much about things like that. I just like to go on gut reaction."

Lisa remembered the hours of work she'd spent on her résumé and getting letters of reference: from her professors at college, from her student-teaching supervisors, and, last of all, from the principal of her school, assuring "to whom it may concern" that Lisa was an excellent teacher, but unfortunately the last hired—therefore, the first to go. So many references, and all of them so very good. Even if he had read them, what difference would it make? All of them were for the wrong job.

"So where did you say you went to school?"

She must focus on her student loans and resist the temptation to remind him he should already know all this.

"Acadia University. In Wolfville. Just an hour away from here. It's an hour west of Halifax too," she added.

"Yes. I know where Wolfville is."

She mustn't show her annoyance at the put-down. She smiled and asked politely, "And where did you get your business degree?"

Whoops. She wasn't supposed to interview him. With luck, he wouldn't notice.

Apparently he didn't; he answered the question. "Business degree? I don't have a business degree. I have an MA in English literature. I've taught a few extension courses for various universities."

How ironic! An unemployed English teacher who wanted to get a job in tourism in a country inn that was an unfinished heap of rubble, and managed by an unemployed English professor. Lisa covered her mouth with her hand, trying to hide the laughter bubbling to her lips.

"Now," Clinton said, "you've found out my qualifications. What are yours? What did you take at Acadia?"

He should understand, but would he? She lowered her hand, paused, and took a deep breath before she answered. "A degree in education. Well, before that, an arts degree. I'm an English teacher, but jobs are very tight, and I thought I might try—" She swallowed hard, then squared her shoulders and looked him straight in the eye. "—might try being a social director."

"I see. You thought you'd try being a social director, did you? While you were about it, why didn't you just run off to New York and try being a brain surgeon? The pay's better, and your qualifications for both equally imaginary."

Well. Well, indeed!

The retort came into her head and out her mouth, and she blurted, "Why shouldn't I have imaginary qualifications? I seem to be applying for an imaginary job at an imaginary inn run by an imaginary manager!"

Error! She'd blown it. After all the hours doing the résumé and putting her dossier together—she'd blown it, simply and purely because she put the mouth in gear before engaging the brain.

She'd no chance of being hired now, even if there'd been a real inn. She started to mumble an apology.

Clinton laughed, showing his firm white teeth. He had dimples on both sides of his mouth, even deeper than hers.

"I like that. Spirit, and honesty, and a sense of humor. Yes, I like that."

Her spirits rose. She beamed.

He stopped laughing.

"I've interviewed several graduates of tourism programs," he said. "They were very boring—lean and bright and all dressed in the same navy blue business suit with a white shirt and sensible navy blue pumps."

Her spirits fell.

"Now," he said. "You told me that teaching jobs were very tight. That's fine, but I understand you were fired from your last one."

"If you didn't read my résumé, how did you know about my last job?"

He shrugged. "I may have glanced at it," he said. "Quit changing the subject. What was your last teaching job, and if you weren't fired, why are you unemployed in the middle of the year?"

"I taught grade twelve English in a small town near the city, for a year and a half," she said, voice crisp. "And I was not fired. The town's main industry shut down, lots of people moved away, the school population declined, and the education funding declined even faster. The school board kept us as long as they could, but at Christmas they laid off several teachers, including me. I've been living on unemployment insurance for the last five months and looking for work, but jobs have been cut everywhere."

He persisted. "Why were you among those let go? In my business, when we have to cut staff, the deadwood goes first."

"No," she said. "That's not the way it works. It goes by seniority. The last people hired were the first let go. Just go back and read my references."

He raised his eyebrows. "That doesn't prove much," he said. "It's often part of the deal. Go quietly, promise you won't make waves, and we'll reward you with good references.''

''That is not the way it was!''

It wasn't likely this tirade would help her get a job either, but really . . . the idea of insulting her by suggesting she'd been fired!

She might as well face it. Her chances of being hired were somewhat less than zero anyway. The other hopefuls had tourism degrees; all she had was expertise at handling teenagers and teaching them to write research papers and enjoy Shakespeare. Neither of the above were useful skills for entertaining guests at a country inn.

She must have been crazy when she thought she could get this job on nothing but imagination and hope.

Clinton slid from his perch. ''Well, Lisa, I think it's time for you to have a tour of this imaginary inn.''

He gestured for her to stand up. As she grabbed for her purse and file folder, she stumbled on her high heels.

Clinton reached out a hand to steady her. Just in time, she caught the purse and file folder and laid them on the desk. The brochure he'd mailed her fluttered down beside them. She recovered it.

His hand still loosely clasped her arm. Her glance locked on his chiseled profile and her natural optimism soared.

Don't be silly, Lisa. He's no nicer than he ever was. You're just relieved at not being thrown out.

He jerked his hand back as if she were a hot stove. ''This way, please.'' He guided her into the embryo dining room and kitchen, pointing out where the stoves and refrigerators, counters and sinks would go. At the moment, the room was empty except for stacks of windows, still in their crates.

''Where are the carpenters? Shouldn't this be a workday?''

"They're on strike," Clinton said. "Illegally. They'll be back. We're supposed to open on July first, but that's only a month away. We might have made it, if they hadn't left."

"What's wrong? Nobody paid them?"

He grinned. "Nobody paid them what they thought they wanted. And nobody's going to. Around here, I decide what the wages are."

"I see." Her voice was so cool she recognized the fact herself.

Stop it, Lisa. She was behaving almost as if she didn't want to get this job.

The voice of reason in the back of her head whispered, *Well, do you?*

No, the voice of pragmatism answered, *but money's money.*

Besides that, the whole caper sounded like a marvelous challenge. Her first day of teaching hadn't been that great either, but by the time she left, her classes threw her an after-school party complete with ice cream and cake, and their parents had demonstrated in front of the school board office.

Clinton led her back across the lobby and down the hallway that turned to her right.

"The staff living quarters are here. As you can see"— and he opened a couple of the doors they passed—"small offices open off the hallway, and behind each office is the room of the employee. Except for mine. Mine's an apartment. It runs across the back of all the rooms. It's L-shaped, quite large, and the only one that's finished. Want to see it?"

"No," she said, "not really." Was she getting the motel manager's version of "Come up and see my etchings"?

She continued, more pleasantly she hoped, "I mean, no thank you. I'd rather see the rest of the inn."

"All right," he said. "Let's have a look at yours then. We'll give you the end room."

Hmm. Did she have a chance at this job? She glowed.

"Uh," he amended, "I mean we'll give the social director the end room."

Her heart sank.

"Let me show it to you." He led her through the hall. The office was about twelve feet square, and empty. It had one plywood window, which would have, if she could have seen through it, overlooked the parking lot.

Clinton opened the connecting door, letting her move before him into the single bedroom, a larger version of the office.

Dust hung suspended in the air, illuminated by a single sunbeam that came in through a knot in the plywood window. It looked like gold dust in a rainbow. Could that be a good omen?

They moved into the east wing of guest rooms. These didn't have interior walls at all—just two-by-fours between the rooms. The aroma of new lumber filled the air.

The windows, now gaping holes, bisected the cement-block walls. Clinton and Lisa stood side by side and leaned out one of the window spaces. She took a deep breath of fresh, clean, outside air. The light, after the dim caverns with weak lightbulbs, dazzled her eyes.

She shut them and imagined the completed rooms, maybe each one a theme room: a cruise ship's cabin, a Victorian noblewoman's boudoir, a bridal suite, a . . .

Buoyed by Clinton's closeness and increasing friendliness, Lisa opened the brochure he had sent her.

She held out a slick publication, featuring an architect's

drawing under the caption *Forget your worries at The Lunenburg Whaler*. The spacious inn in the brochure resembled Tara. It was finished in red brick with white trim. Mature birch and maple trees dotted the landscape of what was now the gravel parking lot. Flowers galore splashed color on rolling green lawns.

The next page showed the view from the back. Between the wings of the motel was a large kidney-shaped swimming pool, and, toward the end where the space was larger, the drawing showed tennis courts.

Right now, Lisa supposed, she and Clinton looked out on the swimming pool.

She pointed to the pool on the drawing.

Clinton gestured at the beginnings of an excavation. An idle backhoe stood to the side.

"There's your swimming pool," he said. "In case you didn't notice, it's imaginary and invisible too, as are the tennis courts just behind it."

They moved to a room on the other side of the hall, stepping over boards and extension cords. "Umm," she said, "the brochure says something about 'close to Nova Scotia's scenic South Shore and the shimmering blue Atlantic.' This, I presume, is where the guests would get the view of the sea if there were one. Where is it? I don't see any sea."

"Oh," he said, "actually, you can glimpse the ocean from the second-story windows." He pointed to the architect's drawing. "If you want a really good look, you can go to the roof. See that little ladder and platform on the top? There's a telescope on the platform."

She leaned out the window and peered up. "What second story?" she asked. "I don't see any second story either."

''Well, actually, the second story's invisible too. We'll build it once the inn becomes wildly successful.''

Huh. Might be a long wait to get a view of the ocean.

They left by the exit door at the end and walked around the building, Lisa stumbling through the dirt in the high heels she'd worn to make a good impression. By time they reached the parking lot in front of the motel, dirt and gravel had worked into her shoes and ground into her hose. She pictured the run creeping up the back of her leg—how elegant.

Maybe he wouldn't notice.

Clinton moved back a step and eyed Lisa, the dust on her shoes, the wide run in her stocking.

True, he should never have let her come, but he had. Now he had to find a way to let her down gently. So far, his cracks about brain surgeons and bright, lean tourism graduates had been of no help. He'd hoped she'd tell him what he could do with his job, but, unfortunately, that hadn't happened.

He couldn't hire her. She didn't know anything about the job she'd applied for. Sure, she was probably a crackerjack English teacher, just as the principal had written, but that didn't help much in the business world. When she stood close to him, she disturbed him in ways he'd determined to avoid while he worked his way up in the business.

He'd do far better to stick with one of the tourism graduates who reminded him of Jennifer.

This enchantress with her big brown eyes and her curves didn't resemble Jennifer in the least. Hiring her and having her working beside him every day was out of the question. Even her quirky sense of humor wasn't quite enough to make him feel safe around her.

When she looked at him he forgot all about his drive to get ahead.

"Shall we go in?" he said.

When they were back in the lobby, he returned to the desk. "Have a seat."

After Lisa sat down, Clinton resumed his spot on the edge of the desk. A little more chat to round out the interview, then send her on her way as gently as possible.

"All right," he said. "You taught English. Anything else?"

"Well, a class of typing one year."

This interested him more than he'd like to admit.

"What else? Extracurricular?"

"Drama. I did drama. You know—directed plays, sewed costumes, taught kids how to build sets."

"I see." He paused. "I still have some other interviews to conduct, and I've already spoken to several qualified applicants. I'll be in touch with you when I've made a decision." It might be easier by mail.

"Don't call us; we'll call you?"

"Well, yes," he said, "I suppose so. But not in the sense you mean. You do have an equal chance with everyone else at this point."

It wasn't a total lie. She had an equal chance with everyone else who had her qualifications.

Chapter Two

Clinton slid from his perch on the desk and held out his hand. Lisa stood and put her hand into his. She didn't want to, but she could hardly refuse to shake hands at the end of a job interview. Sure enough, he held her hand a few seconds too long. She yanked it away.

Even if she should be hired—unlikely—she shouldn't take this job. There wasn't any recreation to direct. The unemployed English professor was trouble. She was much more attracted to him than she should be, and that didn't make for good work relationships.

"Thank you for the interview," she said. "If you decide to hire me, I will do my very best."

"Oh, I'm sure you will, Lisa. I'm sure you will." He paused and his dimple twitched.

The nerve. The nerve of him. The man could read her like a book. She retrieved her belongings and stalked away, head high. *Walk slowly. Don't let him know you're upset.*

17

She marched across the lobby and through the heavy outside door. The sloped ramp angled down more sharply than she'd remembered; the piece of plywood bounced with every step. Her high heels and the gravel in her shoes made control impossible. She found herself gathering momentum until she was running.

As she came to the bottom, one heel caught between the board and the gravel. She sprawled in the dirt, flat on her face, her purse flying in one direction, her file folder in the other, and the contents of the file folder everywhere.

She lay facedown, dirt and gravel in her mouth. The only thing she was angrier about than falling was the possibility that Clinton had seen her. If she could just get out of here without his seeing her—

Too late. She heard footsteps behind her, bounding down the ramp. How humiliating to have him think she was so inept that she couldn't make her way down a simple piece of plywood without falling on her face. Especially humiliating was the thought he might feel sorry for her.

His voice was gentle as he bent over her. "Are you hurt? I'm sorry if you're hurt."

She raised herself on her elbows, and shook her head as if to clear imaginary cobwebs. Heavens, she must look like the Sphinx, lying in the dirt.

"No," she said. "I don't think so." She glared at him. "No thanks to you and your imaginary steps and lawns."

He bent over and put his hands under her arms, lifting her up and propping her on her feet. He did this gently too. But that didn't stop a sudden surge of warmth which swept her from her eyebrows to the pink-polished toes inside her ruined stockings.

This time, he had the grace to ignore his effect on her. "You're a mess, you know."

They both made ineffectual attempts at brushing her off.

"You have a handkerchief in that purse of yours?"

She dug in her pocket and produced a white handkerchief. He reached for it.

"No. I'll take care of it myself."

"Don't be ridiculous," he said. "You can't see properly to do it. Now give." He held out his hand.

"I'm not a dog."

"All right. All right. Please, your majesty, could you please relinquish the handkerchief you are clutching in your hand?"

She sighed. "Here." She handed him the handkerchief and added, "The sarcasm was quite unnecessary."

Holding her head steady with one hand, he wiped her face and her mouth, then stepped back and inspected her. "I think you'd better come back in," he said.

She hesitated. Her self-esteem had already taken enough of a mauling. Any idea of actually getting the job after this display seemed hopeless. Besides, she wasn't sure she wanted to work with him. She remembered how her hand had tingled every time he touched it. To say nothing of the breathless feelings that raced through her when he even looked at her.

Her hesitation was obvious.

"Oh, don't be silly," he said. "I'm not going to hurt you. What sort of person do you think I am?"

There was an awkward silence.

Clinton ran one hand through his hair. Then he said abruptly, "You'd better get back inside that building so you can finish cleaning up. After that, we'll talk more about the job."

What sort of game was he playing? Why had he suddenly

decided to talk further? Did he feel sorry for her? Guilty? Or, most likely, did he think she was going to sue?

She shrugged off his arm, and marched up the ramp and into the lobby. He followed.

"Now," he said, "I think the practical thing would be for you to come into my apartment."

"No!"

He shrugged and disappeared. When he came back, he handed her a towel.

"Here," he said. "Go to your room and clean up."

She went to the end room, washed, and ran a comb through her hair.

She looked over her shoulder and checked her panty hose. By now, they had more ladders than a construction site. She stripped them off and tossed them to join the rest of the debris in a cardboard box containing pieces of gypsum board and cigarette butts and remnants of workers' lunches.

When she returned to the lobby, Clinton was behind his desk.

She cleared her throat.

He stood up, waved her to his chair and leaned against the filing cabinet.

"Look, Lisa," he said, crossing his arms, "may I level with you?"

"Yes. That might be a nice change."

"Okay. You know that your qualifications for this job are less than zero, don't you?"

"Yes."

"But if you'll look around you, you'll see that any need for a social and recreation director is also less than zero."

She didn't answer except to raise her eyebrows.

"However, I do need help in this place." He added abruptly, "You said you taught typing one year. Now, unless you were totally unqualified, that means you can type.''

''Type?''

''Yes, Lisa, type. As in punch those funny little keys and make black marks on white paper.''

She took a deep breath. The nerve of him, thinking she'd teach something she wasn't qualified for. The irony struck her, and she bit back laughter.

''Yes,'' she said. ''I used to type sixty words a minute, but I think it's faster on my laptop.''

Well. At last. She had his attention. His undivided, *respectful* attention.

''You have your own laptop?''

''Yes.''

''It could come with you?''

''Yes.''

''And a printer? You have a printer?''

''Yes,'' she said. ''Just a little one.''

''Uh, you mentioned sewing costumes. That, I guess, means you can sew?''

She chuckled. ''As a matter of fact,'' she said, ''I can. And, yes, I have my own sewing machine.''

This whole interview had taken some very bizarre twists.

''Good,'' he said. ''You're hired.''

''You're serious?''

''Very serious.''

''You needn't hire me out of sympathy or guilt, you know.''

He gave her an exasperated look. ''I'm not hiring you out of sympathy or guilt. Don't be ridiculous!''

She persisted. ''Then why are you hiring me?''

''Because I need a typist and a seamstress. I know I advertised for a social and recreation director. When the time comes I need one of those, I'll see. No promises. At the very best, it's only a seasonal job—we plan to close up for the winter—but, for now, it's yours if you want it.''

Seasonal? She was disappointed, of course. But the alternative appeared to be no job. She'd take it.

Suddenly he smiled a smile that turned her insides into mush. "Let's put it this way—maybe the unemployed teacher, the unemployed professor, and the imaginary country inn just sort of belong together. Let's give it a try, shall we?'' He stepped forward to shake hands, then apparently thought better of it and jammed his hands, knotted into fists, firmly into the pockets of his shorts.

"When do I start?'' she asked.

"Tomorrow.''

"Tomorrow? What on earth am I going to do tomorrow?''

He shrugged, almost as if he regretted his impulsive decision to hire her. "Don't worry. There'll be something.''

"Oh,'' she said. She thought of the total dearth of other people on the grounds. She thought of the way her hand felt when he held it. She remembered that real jobs came with real contracts.

"Could I have something in writing?''

"What do you mean—something in writing?''

"You know—a contract. Whatever.''

"Well,'' he said, "I don't have contracts for nonspecific seasonal jobs, but—if you insist.''

He took a blank sheet of paper from his desk and scribbled something on it, then handed it to her.

This is to confirm that Elizabeth Louise Bannerman has a position at this inn, beginning June 6, and con-

tinuing as long as she's needed or until the inn closes, whichever happens first.

She wrinkled her nose when she read it. It didn't seem much better than no contract at all. However, if she kept pushing, he might forget about feeling guilty and change his mind.

"I suppose I may as well commute for the first while, until things are, uh, more complete?"

He shrugged again. "I wouldn't think so. Things won't ever be more complete if nobody works. Anyway, your office and your room have walls, and the plumbing works—it isn't fancy, but it works."

"And furniture? Where do I sit? Where do I sleep? Where do I hang my clothes?"

He shrugged again. "By tomorrow night, I'll have a cot or something for you." He added, "If you don't like your room, you can share mine."

She drew her breath in, ready to retort.

"Sorry," he said. "Joke."

It had better be a joke. She really needed this job. She really needed any job. But she didn't intend to tolerate harassment. Not of any kind.

"Thank you for hiring me," she said. "I'll see you tomorrow."

Clinton stood in the doorway and watched her go—Elizabeth Louise Bannerman, social and recreation director and jack-of-all-trades.

Not that he hadn't given her the mistaken impression they were in the same boat. He'd told her no lies. He did have a degree in English literature. He had taught some university extension courses years ago. He'd also beat around the country for a few years, working at odd jobs. Finding himself, he supposed it was called.

Probably just as well she didn't know those days were long gone. Let her continue thinking of him as an unemployed English prof.

He cursed himself for his weakness in hiring her. He'd hired her because he couldn't bear to say no. Any self-respecting woman should have told him what he could do with his job, but she'd taken his insults on the chin and snapped right back. He admired courage; he couldn't bear the thought of never seeing her again.

Yes, he needed a typist, but he could have handled that himself on the old beat-up standard. It wasn't as if this place generated a lot of paperwork. By time the inn opened, his office would be outfitted with a complete computerized system.

When Jennifer turned up and scanned the résumés in the filing cabinet, she might think the rural atmosphere had turned his brain.

However, it was a done deed, and, while Jennifer might be boss, he insisted on a free hand whenever he went out on a job. He would put Lisa to work at whatever he could find: his typing, his bookkeeping, the drapes, and any other manual labor that needed doing. If, that is, she ever showed up. He wouldn't send out the letters of rejection to the other applicants. Not quite yet.

He liked what he'd seen of her—her enthusiasm, her imagination, her spirit. Her dimples, her legs, her straight classic nose. Jennifer would not be impressed by dimples and legs and noses. She might be impressed by enthusiasm and imagination.

He'd deal with Jennifer when she got here. In the meantime, this spunky unemployed English teacher might well be willing to help get the inn started in ways the tourism graduates wouldn't think of: with hammers and paintbrushes and sandpaper and scrub buckets. There was a lot to do, and, for a long while yet, none of it had anything to do with social directing.

He wished he didn't feel quite so attracted to her. He had enough on his plate in the next few months without getting himself into romantic entanglements. His number one goal in life was to get out of these boondocks—alone! Hopefully the next new inn would be somewhere like Paris.

By eight in the morning, Lisa had jammed Pink Sally to the ceiling: night table, duvet, laptop and printer, sewing machine, books from the public library, suitcases full of clothes, and a bag lunch—just in case. She needed all these things and more. She needed her own iron. Yes, and her own vacuum cleaner, and her own kitchen table.

She'd have to skip the last two, but she could take an air mattress. The promised cot was undoubtedly as imaginary as everything else around the place.

Remembering her brainstorm about theme rooms, she included a cardboard file of drawings she'd made of stage sets when she was teaching. A few went back to plays she'd worked on in high school and college. If she got up the nerve to suggest this to Clinton, some of these sketches might furnish her with ideas.

At the last minute, she threw in a dozen romance novels for whiling away the solitary evenings.

When she arrived at the inn, she was surprised to see Clinton come bounding down the ramp

"Hi," she said, opening the car door.

"Hi. Thought I'd come out and help you carry your things."

He tucked her night table under one arm, and carried the duvet and laptop with the other hand while she trotted behind, toting suitcases.

The room was exactly as it had been yesterday. The only object in it was the box full of plasterboard ends and workmen's cigarette butts and her own torn panty hose. The promised cot was indeed as imaginary as the view.

"Hmm," Clinton said as he set down the night table, "you seem to have brought everything but the kitchen sink."

Lisa snorted. "It looks as if I should have brought that too! Not likely there's one in residence!"

"Well, there you are," he said as he set the computer and the rolled-up duvet on the floor.

"Ah," he said. "Nice laptop."

She surveyed the room and Clinton, hands on hips. "What's the big deal about the laptop? Every business these days has a computer. Sounds as if you don't even have anything to type on."

He shrugged. "Depends on your definition, I guess. I've got an old Underwood if you don't mind spending half your time untangling sticky keys and the other half going blind trying to see what you've typed. I'll get a personal computer in here someday."

She just bet he would. As soon as he finished paying for that charming secondhand filing cabinet. She was getting a better idea about this place and its manager with every passing second.

However, a job was a job. She'd never yet taken money from an employer without giving her best effort in return.

"Now, what do you want me to do?"

He shrugged and equivocated. "There'll be something.

You'd better spend the first few hours getting unpacked and settling in.''

"Do you have a broom," she badgered, "and a dustpan, and some old rags?"

"Oh. Room not clean enough for you?"

"That's right," she said, hands on hips, "it's not!"

"See what I can find." He left.

She was sitting on the floor blowing up her air mattress when he returned.

"Here," he said as he came through the doorway, holding a broom, a dustpan, and a handful of rags. "I found some."

"About time," she muttered as she looked up, her face red.

He hit his forehead with the heel of his hand when he saw what she was doing. "I promised you a cot."

"Yes, you did!"

"Here." He moved over to her. "At least let me help you."

He sat on the floor beside her, and took the air valve away from her. He blew into it without effort. She'd rapidly become out of breath and red in the face. The mattress lay in her lap, and, as he bent over, she looked down on the back of his head and the nape of his neck. The mahogany hair curled over his forehead and down on his neck, but was, in spite of the surroundings, clean and shiny.

She started to reach her hand out to stroke his hair, then jerked it back when she realized what she'd almost done. Not enough oxygen reaching the brain, obviously.

When she moved her hand down to sit on it and keep it out of trouble, it brushed against the side of his leg, sending a little jolt of electricity through her. Hopefully, he hadn't noticed. She moved both hands to the floor, and sat on them.

She continued to look down at him. There wasn't anywhere else to look unless she stared at the ceiling or the wall. The shoulders beneath his tank top bulged, and the mattress firmed up quickly. Clinton's breath came and went as easily as normal breathing. He inserted the plug that kept the air from escaping.

"There you are," he said again as he got to his feet. "I'll leave you to your cleaning."

Clinton walked back to his desk. Better and better. She'd not only supplied her own computer and sewing machine, but her own bed and furniture. The woman appeared to be capable of coping with any situation—except, perhaps, himself. He'd felt the delicate touch of her hand brushing his thigh, and the embarrassed recoil.

He'd have liked the touch to linger, and wished again that this had not been so. She wasn't the type to toy with, even if she weren't his employee; she'd already touched his heart too much for a casual flirtation.

Lisa was the kind of woman you took home to meet the family, the kind of woman for serious intentions.

He'd no intention of getting serious about anyone for several years, not until he was established professionally, and located in one place. The only woman he'd ever considered marrying had convinced him of that.

"*Oh, yes, Clinton,*" Samantha had told him. She was sure it was all very exciting driving a logging truck in Alaska, working on a salmon boat off the coast of British Columbia, building houses in Yellowknife. But it didn't really add up to a family life, did it, Clinton? With that she'd pulled the ring off her finger, deposited it on his palm, and left.

He wasn't about to try again with a woman until he had a future to offer her that didn't included traipsing around North America from one near-bankrupt inn to another.

He shook his head to clear out these intrusive and un-welcome thoughts.

After all, he'd met Lisa only yesterday.

Once Clinton left, Lisa did some deep breathing exercises to calm her erratic pulse. Why did the man have this effect on her? He was rude and boorish and overbearing and she loathed him. Of course, she did.

She got to her feet, dusted off the back of her jeans, and picked up the broom. What wouldn't sweep up, she took damp rags to.

When she finished, she looked at her little heap of be-longings, at the night table, and at the air mattress and duvet spread out on the floor. It didn't compare with either her old bedroom at home or with the recent apartment she'd had to give up.

She remembered her long-ago teenage fantasies, when she'd pretended she was Elizabeth Louise, tall and blond, with ice-blue eyes and a velvet-draped four poster. This didn't exactly compare with that either.

She chuckled to herself. No point being maudlin. She'd make the best of what she had. At least her new room was clean and it was hers. She sat on the air mattress and ate her ham sandwich and drank her lukewarm container of V8 juice.

After she finished eating, she looked around. There wasn't anything else she could do here. Reluctantly, she scrambled to her feet, dragged the box of junk out into the hallway, gathered the broom, dustpan, and rags together, and set out to return them to the lobby.

Clinton sat at his desk, his head bent over columns of figures. He still wore the tank top and khaki shorts, but the sandals had been exchanged for steel-toed construction boots.

"Here are your things," she said.

"What things?" he asked without looking up.

"The broom and dustpan."

"Oh. Just put them anywhere."

She propped them against a cement-block wall and laid the rags on the floor beside them.

"Well," she said, "there's something else. Is there anything in particular you want me to do? Anything you want typed right now?"

"No. Nothing I need typed."

"Or sewn?"

"No. Nothing I need sewn either."

"But, uh, you said, that is, you hired me—"

"Yes, I mentioned typing and sewing as two possibilities. Your contract just said 'a position,' nonspecific. We've got an inn to open, and the carpenters are all on strike. You and I are going to Sheetrock and plaster and paint. Right now you're holding Sheetrock for me."

Lisa drew herself up, curled her hands into fists, placed them on her hips, and leaned forward.

"Oh, no," she said, "oh, no. I won't do that kind of work. You hired me as a secretary, and maybe someday a social director."

"I didn't hire you for anything specific," he said. "Your contract says you have a job as long as you're needed. Well, today you're needed for carpentry. Besides that, you said you coached drama, including teaching students how to build sets. That sounds like related job experience to me.''

''No, it's not the same at all. Teaching set design was artistic. The total package. I was creating something that would add to the whole illusion of the play.''

''Whatever.''

''Huh. I've a good mind to just leave.'' She shook her head for emphasis, and repeated, ''I won't do that type of work.''

He gave her a mocking look.

''Oh, yes, you will. You'll do that kind of work. Those uppity types with their business suits and their tourism degrees wouldn't have. But Lisa will. Lisa needs a job. Isn't that true?''

Lisa sighed and thought of her car payments. Yes, it was true. But it was still humiliating to realize he'd hired her because she was so unqualified she'd agree to be a jack-of-all-trades.

Sometime she'd like to get back to doing work *she* wanted to do, professional work, work that six years of college and fourteen months of experience had qualified her for. Sometime she'd like to snap her fingers in a man's face and say, ''Hold your own Sheetrock!''

This wouldn't be the time. She needed the job too badly. She'd do the jobs that weren't important enough for him: she'd dust his filing cabinet, she'd fetch his coffee; she'd hold his wallboard. At least until she found a better job.

''But,'' she said, ''what about crossing picket lines?''

''See any picket lines around? I told you it was an illegal walkout, not an official strike.''

Lisa took her fists off her hips, crossed her arms, and let her body slump back. Yes, she'd do it, but that didn't mean she had to like it. Or like *him*. The arrogant, obnoxious—

"Come on," he said. "Let's get on with our manual labor. I was just waiting for you to be ready."

"All right," she said. "You win. Where's the hammer?"

"Here we are," Clinton said after she'd followed him into the east wing. "The supplies are here. It's where the carpenters left off. Now, it would have been slow going for me to do this alone, but all I want you to do is hold the Sheetrock while I nail. It's necessary, but it's not hard, and it's not going to give you aches where you didn't know you had muscles."

He put on a carpenter's apron, filled it with nails from the box on the floor, and hung a hammer from it. Then he picked up a full sheet of wallboard and carried it to the first stretch of wall as easily as if it had been an empty carton.

Lisa was impressed in spite of herself. When she'd taught and supervised set designing, she'd always called on her personal army of teenaged football players for the heavy fetching and carrying. An unemployed professor, with muscles yet, and some sort of knowledge of manual skills—and broad shoulders and narrow waist and hips and . . .

He moved the Sheetrock into place.

"Here," he said. "All I want you to do is stand against it so it can't fall over or move while I nail it. Can you do that?"

Could she do that? Of course she could do that. Any seven-year-old child could do that. But it wasn't why she spent six years in college.

She stood with her back to the wall, leaning against the sheet of wallboard, feet braced several inches out.

''Piece of cake,'' she said aloud. She might as well pretend to be a good sport about it.

That was before he leaned right over her to nail above her head. His chest almost touched her nose. She smelled the clean male smells of sweat and construction sites. A hole in the shirt right at eye level gave a close-up view of bronzed pectoral muscles.

Her heart hammered so loudly she imagined the sound echoing, bouncing off his chest. Fortunately he seemed to have no idea of the effect he was having on her, and in a few minutes he said, ''Okay. On to the next.''

The work moved quickly. By the end of the afternoon, they'd finished four rooms, except for ceilings, and, in spite of herself, she felt a glow of pride in work well done. She wasn't going to admit that to him.

''Well,'' she said caustically, ''another forty-four rooms and we'll be finished.''

''I hope the carpenters will be back long before that,'' he said. ''But it's just as well for them to realize that work can go on without them.''

He looked at her dust-covered jeans and shirt. ''You've done good work this afternoon. Go change and I'll buy you a hamburger. I owe you that much.''

Lisa changed into clean jeans, and a red silk shirt that set off her dark hair and eyes.

A hamburger, Clinton had said.

What if? What if her jeans and shirt had been satin evening wear and her leather sneakers matching pumps? What if the promised hamburger were, instead, filet mignon? What if Clinton Daniels were not her employer, but the manager of a neighboring hotel? What if he'd been dressed in a dark suit and tie and a shirt so white it dazzled?

What if . . .

Lisa snorted at her own fantasies. She'd obviously been out of work and out of circulation too long.

He owed her the hamburger. He'd been right about that. From the looks of this place, it might well be the only payment she'd ever get.

As for having any interest in Clinton Daniels— That idea deserved a triple snort. Oh, yes, she'd trembled at his touch. That just went to show the only man she'd seen lately had been her father.

The June air was soft and warm as they drove inland to a small café. The building was a simple A-frame with a warm, welcoming interior of knotty pine.

There were few other customers, so after hamburgers and fries and three cups of coffee, Clinton and Lisa lingered at their wooden table with its cheerful Wedgwood-blue top. Little woven baskets sitting on each table held triangular pegboard games. Lisa toyed with one of these as she and Clinton chatted.

She told him about her home, that her mother was a housewife, and that her dad taught science in a Halifax high school. He'd been with the same school all his working life, and was looking forward to a comfortable retirement in a few more years.

She told him about herself: school, classes, piano lessons, team sports, cheerleading, figure skating, drama. That was just high school. Although it had happened a very long time ago, Clinton seemed interested in everything. In fact, he drew her out to talk about things almost forgotten, including the fact that at one point, after she'd won a couple of regional championships, she'd actually considered the idea of becoming a professional figure skater.

Why he showed so much interest in all this was a major

mystery, but it would be much better for her future if her boss became her friend rather than a cross between Simon Legree and Red Riding Hood's wolf.

He appeared much less threatening now that his body was decently covered in blue jeans and an off-white cotton shirt.

"And at Acadia?" he prompted. "Were you in all of this sort of thing there too?"

"Well, lots of things, but different ones from high school. Except for drama. I didn't take lessons or compete in figure skating anymore, but I did work with the younger skaters as a volunteer coach. Then, when we were student teaching, there wasn't much time for anything else. I enjoyed it," she said.

"And the teaching itself?"

She glowed with enthusiasm. "I loved it. I just loved it. I love teens, and it was exciting teaching them the writing and research skills they'd need in the future, and I loved proving to them that poetry and Shakespeare can be fun."

"You must have been disappointed with the cutbacks and layoffs."

She looked across the table at him. "I was devastated," she said. "And not just about the money." She shrugged. "But no point in moping around, is there? You go on."

"You don't want to hang in and wait for things to improve?"

"Hah! I might still be waiting when I'm eighty, and my brand new car's a heap of rust, and I'm in jail for never repaying my student loans."

"You haven't considered working at what substitute teaching you can get until things open up?"

"Yeah, if I'd been an elementary-school teacher I might have done that. But going in one day for physics? Another for

French? On twenty minutes' notice? Huh-uh. I don't want to do it if I can't do it well.''

She blushed faintly. Fortunately he didn't connect the remark to her rash attempt to become a recreation director with neither training nor experience.

She paused and ran the peg from the game around the perimeter of the board.

''On to a new life. Who knows, once I get into it I might find that the Lunenburg Whaler is a lot of fun too. Then I won't have to worry about things getting better in teaching unless *you* lay me off.''

She remembered the seasonal nature of her new job. She chuckled so he wouldn't think she'd been angling for better treatment. ''Whoops. Forgot my contract. Guess that might happen sooner rather than later.''

''We'll cross that bridge when we come to it,'' Clinton said. ''For now, we'll both do what needs doing. When the carpenters get back, I'll start you typing letters and doing the books. Maybe sewing. You did bring your sewing machine?''

''Uh-huh. Don't you remember? You carried it in. On your third trip.''

He twitched his eyebrows and looked at her from his hazel eyes. ''Guess that slipped my mind. I moved in so many pieces of furniture, I lost track. Anyway, I hired you because you could type and sew. I'll have you sew the drapes,'' he added. ''I'll pay for the material with what I save on one room.''

She'd just bet he would. She'd furnished an apartment recently enough to have an idea of what drapes cost. He'd probably pay her total season's salary with what he'd save altogether.

''That's fine,'' she said. What else could she say? She really needed this job.

He gave her a lazy grin. ''You're a good sport, Lisa,'' he said. ''You take imaginary inns and views and swimming pools all in your stride.''

Chapter Three

Lisa returned to jumping and removing pegs on the triangular board. When she could go no further, she carved ridges in her paper napkin with long red fingernails. "Oh," she said, "I guess I've always had a lot of imagination. Comes in handy teaching."

She wrinkled her nose. Clinton was nice. His hazel eyes had gold flecks that made them look warm and friendly. How could she ever have thought of them as yellow wolf's eyes?

"You're very close to your parents. You've always lived at home?"

"Oh, no. Of course not. I was at Acadia for six years. I lived in the dorm four years, and since then I've had an apartment. But when I lost my job, it seemed sensible to move back home. Sure, I can collect unemployment, but how far does that go? And for how long?"

She changed the subject. "And what about you? Where did you go to school, et cetera?"

"Well, I'm somewhat like you—an only child of doting parents. Probably more spoiled than you, at first, though the wheels sort of came off the family wagon of indulgence when I spent a few years after high school roaming around and doing odd jobs for a living. Then, when I did decide to go to college, I opted for English literature rather than business. I took my first degree at Acadia too."

"Did you really? What on earth brought you to Acadia?"

"Well, I was still pretty immature, and wanted to do the opposite of whatever the family expected. The options were to continue drifting around western Canada or going away to school. I'd never been east of Montreal, so instead of continuing to 'go west, young man,' I thought I'd try the East for a change."

"And?"

"My family determined I should get a business degree and then an MBA, eventually taking over the family business. But I was a rebel and I majored in English literature, because I couldn't find anything my parents considered more useless.

"I found I liked the East, and, regardless of my motives in taking it up, I also liked English literature. I hadn't completely outgrown my rebel stage, so I did an MA, and then started looking for jobs. English profs are as abundant and redundant as high-school teachers, so here I am."

"Yes. Well," Lisa said, "I guess maybe life always went a bit too smoothly for me. Up till five months ago, anyway." She smiled. "You know, my mother used to say

I saw the world as one big swimming pool, created just so I could sit by it in a bikini.''

Clinton watched her speculatively. She blushed.

He looked away and continued talking.

"My dad cut off the funding because I wouldn't follow the corporate agenda. Summers I worked at whatever I could—carpenter's helper a couple of summers, which is coming in handy now. I worked on road crews, and put in one summer as a short-order cook out in Jasper.''

"Mm," she said. "Sounds more interesting than frying hamburgers at McDonald's.'' That was how she'd earned extra money in high school and college. "But how did all this lead to being manager of a motel near Chester, Nova Scotia?"

He shifted in his seat and examined the table. "Well, I like this area, so when I had a chance at this job I took it. Shall we just say I've given up the fight? Poverty isn't as appealing at almost thirty as it was at twenty.''

Huh! Interesting story. But the way he'd refused to meet her eyes at the end made her think he'd probably left some things out.

He finished the pegboard game and threw the triangle back into its little basket. They stood up and left the restaurant.

By then, it was dark. The air was heavy with spring, and the moon was full. Clinton reached for Lisa's hand and stroked the back of it with the ball of his thumb.

"Any fiancés or boyfriends?'' he asked as they walked to the car.

"No one special. And you?''

"Nobody special," he said.

She'd found out a lot about him, some of it possibly the truth, but she still didn't know how he'd become manager of The Lunenburg Whaler. She doubted he was about to share that information with her at any time in the near future.

A few miles to the south, the road crossed a small river with rapids pouring over rocks. Clinton pulled onto the shoulder and parked.

Perhaps she should object. But why? All they were doing was sitting in a car, enjoying the evening. They sat for a few moments listening to the rushing water, watching the glimmer of the moon.

"Ah," Clinton said. "Beautiful night, isn't it?"

"Very beautiful."

He laid one arm across the back of the seat. Lisa had seen the script for this show before. She shifted slightly away, wedging her back firmly into the angle between the seat and the front door.

If that was his game, he was about to be disappointed. She needed this job, and joining the manager in extracurricular activities would be the fastest way to lose it.

He brought his arm down to where he could touch and caress her shoulder.

There was no further place to run, figuratively speaking, and still stay in the car.

"No," she said.

He withdrew his hand. "No? On a moonlit night overlooking a river. No?"

"No, Clinton. I came here to work, not play games. Now, if you'd just get that wandering arm and its semiattached fingers back somewhere in the vicinity of the steering wheel . . ."

He did. Quickly. "You're not a lot of fun," he said.

"I didn't come here to be fun. I came here to work and

earn money. I have student loans and a hefty car payment. Maybe after those, I'll think about fun.''

''Promises, promises.'' He started the car, and eased it back onto the road. ''I guess it's time to get you back anyway if you're going to be in shape to hold plasterboard tomorrow.''

They drove back through the moon-drenched night. As they entered the inn, she touched his cheek with gentle fingers, and stood on tiptoe to give him a brief good-night kiss, a sisterly, ''thanks for the nice time, I hope we're still friends'' kind of kiss.

But somehow, Clinton moved his head so that the lips intended for his cheek landed on his mouth instead. Somehow, Lisa's breathing quickened, and the hand she had laid softly against his shoulder made its way around his neck. Somehow, when Clinton kissed her back, not briefly, nor brotherly, she let him, encouraged him, joined him.

Her pulse throbbed. When Clinton tightened his arms around her, sanity returned.

Innocent intentions and all, she couldn't deny she'd started it. She edged herself backward, out of his arms, and laughed lightly to pretend the whole thing was nothing.

''Thank you for tonight, Clinton,'' she said, a bit breathlessly. ''It was truly lovely, but I won't forget tomorrow that you're the boss, and I'm the carpenter's helper!''

Later as she snuggled down in her duvet on the air mattress, she still felt Clinton's kiss on her lips.

Stupid. She'd been plain stupid, had kept him at arm's length all evening and then at the end had behaved like a thoughtless silly girl, not like the professional woman she was.

Well, she'd have to be sure she didn't let her guard down again.

Clinton shut his apartment door behind him. Stupid of him to have made moves there in the moonlight by the river and to have spent the drive home wishing he'd been more successful.

Then it had been even more stupid to have deliberately misunderstood her casual kiss, what was obviously no more than a "thank you for the nice evening" kind of kiss, a hamburger kind of kiss.

Like a fool, he'd turned it into a champagne-and-roses kind of kiss.

He was attracted to her—no doubt about it, had been since that first day he'd heard her voice on the phone asking if she could send in her résumé.

But to kiss her? He hadn't even been lucky enough for the kiss to kill his interest. It had been more like the salad at a banquet—fresh and green and stimulating hunger for the coming feast.

That was all very well, but there could be no coming feast; in fairness, he must let Lisa know that. Would she have gotten the wrong idea? Mistaken an ill-advised impulse for a sincere interest?

They had to work together for several months; it wouldn't do for her to imagine he was in love with her nor even seriously attracted.

To her, that kiss might have meant that he was interested, that he'd like to continue, to build a relationship, a commitment.

He'd had that problem in the past, women who had tried to use a few kisses as blackmail to further a relationship, to, through those few kisses, build bridges to the family fortune. Fortunately, Lisa didn't know about the family fortune, nor how close his ties to it were. Just the same, better to spell out the guidelines, very clearly, and right now.

The story he'd fed her about his past? There were no lies in it. Just a few omissions. He'd done the things he said he'd done. No need to tell her these things were as long ago as her wannabe figure-skating career.

Tomorrow, if the carpenters were back, he'd take her with him to Bridgewater. He had to buy furniture for her room and have it delivered, and order furniture and supplies for the inn, and buy material for the drapes.

Then he and she would do some sight-seeing and go out to dinner. There, at a restaurant, with the privacy that comes in crowds, and with other people around so that the conversation would have to remain civilized, he would explain the situation to her.

Next morning, the carpenters were back. Lisa and Clinton left them to their carpentering and went to shop in Bridgewater, discussing furniture styles and colors for drapes. Afterward, they went to a Chinese restaurant. They ordered. The food came. They ate.

Lisa watched Clinton. He relapsed into a moody silence. He scowled at his egg roll, frowned at his sweet-and-sour chicken, and looked daggers at his garlic spareribs. By the time the bill and the fortune cookies came his mood still hadn't improved.

Lisa broke her fortune cookie in two and withdrew the tiny slip of paper. "Oh, listen," she said, welcoming the excuse to end the long silence. "My fortune says, 'You are about to strike home runs in work and in love.' Isn't that exciting? What does yours say?"

Clinton looked at his fortune. He looked at Lisa as if he hated her.

She smiled at him expectantly. "Go on. What does it say?"

He crumpled up the tiny piece of paper and said, "Plain speaking now saves misunderstanding later." He cleared his throat and looked uncomfortable. "Listen, Lisa, we have to talk."

He's going to fire me. I'm not good enough. He's mad because I let him kiss me; he's mad because I stopped; he's mad because—

"Yes?" she said.

"Lisa—" He hesitated, looked even more uncomfortable, and covered his confusion by counting out exact change onto the tray with the bill, and adding extra for the tip. "I hope you won't take this the wrong way. About last night—"

So it was about last night.

"I don't really know how to say this," he mumbled.

She put her elbows on the table, propped her chin on her hands, and took a deep breath. "So—just say it."

"All right. I will." He hurtled ahead. "I know that some women can translate one kiss into a proposal of marriage. I just want to make clear that with me a kiss is just a kiss. I don't intend to marry you—"

Lisa let her held breath out with a long hiss, and her voice rose to a crescendo. "What?" she yelped. "Marry you? Why, I wouldn't marry you if you were the last man on earth!"

Heads turned their way.

Clinton held his own voice down to a stage whisper. "No, Lisa, you've got it all wrong. I don't want to marry you."

She pushed her chair back and sat up very straight, arms akimbo, and used her most scathing voice, oblivious of her audience. "Well, it's a good thing, isn't it, because I sure don't want to marry you. And to what do I owe this fascinating revelation?"

He leaned toward her, across the table, no longer bothering to lower his voice. "You owe it to the fact that women don't seem to understand men don't want a serious relationship with every woman they kiss. I'm happy as I am; I don't want a serious relationship with you; I don't want a serious relationship with anybody for at least another ten years, if ever! Just don't take one kiss so seriously."

"Oh!" she sputtered and stood up. "Oh! You conceited jerk. I've kissed more men than you have gray cells in your empty head." She emphasized the words by pounding the fist of one hand into the palm of the other. "A lot more!" She hit her palm again. "And I would marry any one of them before I'd marry you, even the ones from ten years ago who were sixteen, with pimples." She reached for her purse and prepared to flounce out, surreptitiously scooping up Clinton's discarded fortune-cookie paper.

What on earth about that little piece of paper had upset him so?

The restaurant crowd burst into applause. Clinton, apparently seeing the humor in the scene, stood and bowed and waved before he grabbed Lisa's wrist and dragged her out of the restaurant.

When they were seated in the car, he said, "Look, I'm sorry about that. I just wanted you to understand that I'm not into marriage."

Her anger had blown itself out. She looked out the window as the car began to move. She watched the houses and lights of Bridgewater go by.

''That's all very well, but what on earth inspired you to think I was?'' She added, ''Do I still have a job?''

He grinned. ''I don't know. I hired you to type and sew. Can you still type and sew?''

''I think so.''

Clinton turned his attention to the highway, and Lisa sneaked a look at the slip of paper in her fingers.

You have just met the girl of your dreams.

Clinton stared at the road. She was so cute when she was mad. Not that he was going to become involved, cute or not. If he'd been able to resist all the cool beauties who'd crossed his path in the last few years, he certainly wasn't going to become infatuated with some little spitfire with the hairstyle of a cairn terrier and the temperament of a Siamese cat!

However, he'd fumbled the ball on this scrimmage, and he couldn't blame her for getting annoyed. She was still talking to him, she was still willing to type and sew, and she apparently hadn't considered one kiss a proposal of marriage.

Still, she'd shown a lot of enthusiasm for her own fortune cookie. *Home runs in love and in work.* Huh. Is that what it really said? Had she made it up on the spur of the moment and blurted it out to him to test the waters?

They'd have to have a serious discussion about this, sometime soon when he'd thought about what he should say a lot more carefully than he had today.

You have just met the girl of your dreams. Ha!

When they returned to the inn, Lisa walked through the door of her room with her arms full of material, followed by Clinton with two table lamps, a card table, and parcels.

She bumped the light switch with her elbow; she gasped. First, there *was* a light, an actual ceiling fixture that gave off a soft white glow.

Dusty rose carpet covered the floor. The walls were painted off-white. A real window with real drapes replaced the plywood. Her new furniture was set up: a full bed complete with mattresses and pillows, a dresser, a desk, a couple of chairs, all in light oak, and a beige metal filing cabinet.

It still wasn't in the same league as the luxurious four-poster bed and fashionable furniture belonging to the Elizabeth Louise of her youthful dreams, but it was much closer to the real rooms she'd lived in than it had been this time yesterday.

Clinton tossed the parcels onto one of the beds. Lisa watched him leave and pondered on the day.

Clinton had done this for her—Clinton who'd teased and tormented her when they first met, who'd *forgotten* to get her the promised cot, who'd totally humiliated her in the restaurant earlier tonight. Was he sweet and considerate, or was he arrogant and rude?

Whatever he was, he wasn't dull!

At 7:30 next morning, Lisa wandered out to the lobby, to find Clinton already there, talking with a man in a hard hat. All around were the cheerful sounds of hammers and power saws. The man in the hard hat disappeared, and Clinton turned to Lisa.

She greeted him with a mock salute and a cheerful smile. " 'Morning, Boss. What's on for today? Do I start sewing, or is there something else?"

"The first thing that's on is breakfast. I hoped this was the day I could lure you to my lair." His leer was as fake as the salute she'd given him. ''There are at least ten men about, ready to rush to your rescue when the first faint scream leaves your maidenly lips.''

''Okay, okay.'' She raised her hands in an exaggerated gesture of conciliation. ''You've made your point. Not that they'd hear a fire siren over that noise. I'll come, I'll come.''

Clinton's apartment was the typical bachelor pad: tidy, utilitarian, bare.

''Make yourself at home,'' he said, as he busied himself in the tiny kitchen. Lisa wandered into the living room. A sofa bed and matching recliner were covered in blue nylon. A board-and-brick bookcase, a cabinet full of sound equipment, and a television completed the furnishings.

She examined the bookcase. It held many of the classics, as well as books by modern novelists and playwrights.

The tantalizing smell of bacon began to fill the air. She sniffed appreciatively and moved across to the pictures on top of the television. There were a lot—some framed, some propped—pictures of Clinton skiing, pictures of Jasper Lodge, a picture of a slim middle-aged blond woman and a balding thickset man—his mother and father, she presumed.

Lisa looked at the pictures casually. Clinton moved over and stood behind her.

She pointed at one of the pictures. ''You look good on skis.''

''Thank you.''

''The people are friends from Toronto, are they?''

He placed his hands on her shoulders.

''Um. Could be,'' he said. He began to rotate his thumbs over her shoulder blades, sending lovely currents of feeling coursing through her shoulders. ''Which people?''

His hands on her shoulders made it very hard to concentrate on the pictures or anything else. She wriggled her
shoulder blades. Abruptly Clinton moved away, as if he'd
just become aware of what he was doing.

"Well," she said, pointing, "there's the blond woman
with the man. Your parents?"

"Huh-uh," he said. "My parents aren't into pictures.
That's Jennifer and Silas Masters. Remember? My bosses.
They own this place—and a whole chain of others."

Hmm, a little unusual to have a picture of your bosses
in your living room. *She* didn't display pictures of her ex-
principal. Nor of the people who owned McDonald's either,
and they had a whole chain of others too.

He seemed disconcertingly aware of his effect on her.
There was laughter in his voice when he said, "Anything
else?"

She shrugged. "The one of Jasper Lodge?"

He laughed aloud. "The one of Jasper Lodge? Oh, yes,
that one. Well, as it happens, that's a picture of Jasper
Lodge. Time to eat."

He led her toward the small table at the kitchen end of
the living room, and held out a chair while she sat down.
He had set the table with blue place mats and matching
napkins, and cheerful yellow plates. Cheese omelets were
already on the plates, coffee was poured, and a platter
heaped with bacon and buttered toast was in the middle of
the table.

"Mmm, good," she said as she tasted the omelet and
helped herself to bacon and toast.

It was very difficult to be stiff and formally polite when
faced with bacon, cheese omelet, and toast dripping with
butter—to say nothing of Clinton sitting across from her,

smiling at her, golden flecks lighting up his hazel eyes—but she gave it her best effort.

"You have a lot of good books," she said.

"Yes," he said. "You may borrow any of them you like. I recommend the works of Shaw. He has very interesting ideas, some of them remarkably up-to-date, about relationships between men and women."

She couldn't let him think he had the upper hand.

"I agree," she said. "I especially like the play where Cleopatra arrives gift-wrapped in a carpet and makes fools of every man in the place."

When Lisa had polished off the last piece of toast, and folded her napkin into a neat square, she stood. If Clinton Daniels imagined she wanted to be anything to him but a recreation director, he was badly mistaken. From now on, she would be all business, strictly business.

"Thank you for the lovely breakfast," she said in a prim and proper schoolteacher voice, then made her way back to the bookcase. She already had a sound knowledge of Shaw and Shakespeare. Her Ibsen was rustier. She picked up a volume that included *A Doll's House* and said, "And now, unless there's something else, I'll start my sewing."

"Well, actually," he said. "There is something else. Why don't I pour you a second cup of coffee, and we'll sit back and talk for a few minutes."

She sat down again and watched him pour the coffee. She looked at him and raised her eyebrows inquisitively. "Yes?"

He ran a hand through his reddish-brown hair.

"Lisa," he said. "I like you. I like you a lot. And I really enjoyed our kiss the other night. So much I'd like a repeat performance many times. But what I like and what I intend to do are two very different things."

"Go on."

"I handled this conversation very badly last night, and I'm sorry. I know I told you that before, but I am. I really am."

He paused. She stayed silent. No way she'd help him out with this.

"Look. I just want to give you my expectations. Just to avoid misunderstandings. What happened the other night won't lead anywhere, and it won't be repeated. As long as you know that."

Lisa opened her mouth to protest; Clinton lifted his hand. "No. I'm not saying you'd assume that, or that you'd want that. But some women do, and it can lead to problems. I can't commit myself to a woman for several more years."

"Um," Lisa said, "I'm not personally interested, you do understand, but, theoretically speaking, just out of curiosity, so to speak, why on earth not? You told me you were almost thirty."

"Because I happen to have the rather old-fashioned idea that I will not ask a woman to share my life until I can stay in one place and take care of her and whatever family might follow."

She raised her eyebrows a little higher, and took several sips from her coffee mug before she answered. "Take care of your wife? In this day and age, she's not going to work?"

"I didn't say that. If she gets fulfillment from working, she can work. But she will not *have* to work. There's a difference."

"I see." She assumed a chilly tone. "Speaking just theoretically, you know, nothing personal, but I've always assumed I would work side by side with my husband to build our home and take care of our family."

"But your mother doesn't work. You told me that. You told me your mother was a housewife."

"Because she preferred it that way. Not because Daddy kept her in a cage. Besides—Mom was part of a different generation."

"Well, anyway," Clinton said, "that's the way I feel about it. So I'd like to continue as friends as long as you understand we'll never be anything more. Ever."

He hesitated a moment, and ran his hand through his hair again. "I don't intend to make a pass at you either, if that's worrying you."

"Oh," she said. "Oh, you don't, don't you? And I suppose this is all your choice. If you *chose* to make a pass at me, I would fall gleefully into your arms. But considering I'm just your humble servant, the lord of the manor won't take advantage of my helpless position. And I have absolutely no choice about whether I'd like it." She added hurriedly, "Not that I would, you understand. This is all theoretical."

Her voice swelled with indignation. "Well, Clinton Daniels, just let me tell you something. This is not the nineteenth century. Poor little servant girls aren't at the beck and call of their employers. I do not have to depend on your gentlemanly instincts for protection. Not even if you had any. You, or any other man, just try laying one finger on me without my permission, and you'll have lawyers swarming over you so fast you'll think your backhoe hit you. Car loans or no car loans.

"Yes, Clinton, you are quite right. You are not going to make a pass at me."

"Lisa," Clinton said. "Please. Let's not quarrel. I just wanted to discuss this as friends, to get everything up front."

She blinked. "I'm sorry." She touched his hand, then snatched her own back. "Sorry I got carried away with that tirade, I mean. Maybe I did overreact. I'm not worried about your intentions and I don't need your protection, from you or from anybody else. But it's all right. I'll remember that you are not going to marry nor seduce me, and I assure you the feeling is quite, quite mutual. Therefore, I don't think we have anything to quarrel about, do we? Now, if you don't mind, I'd just like to borrow this volume of Ibsen before I go."

"Oh, yes," he said. "By all means, borrow the Ibsen. You might even learn something from it. It's about a woman who had everything—absolutely everything: a doting husband, lovely children, servants. She threw it all away because she thought her husband's protectiveness meant he considered her a pet dog instead of a person."

"I know what it's about," she said. "After all, I'm an English major too. It's just that it's been a while since I read it, and I thought I'd refresh my memory."

She patted her lips with her napkin, got up from the table, tucked Henrik Ibsen under her arm, and left.

Chapter Four

Clinton cleared the table and piled the dirty dishes in the sink.

So Lisa believed in the concept of both partners with their shoulders to the wheel, did she? She probably thought she was telling the truth. Until the first time she wanted a new car, and none was forthcoming. Until she realized the next-door neighbor had a bigger diamond. Not that he'd have the trouble supporting a wife, new cars and bigger diamonds included, that Lisa might have assumed he would.

He'd misled her a bit there. It didn't matter. He'd gotten his message across. He should be pleased. Lisa had received the message loud and clear. The question was, had he? He must. He intended to stay free of emotional involvements for at least another six years. If he wanted to join the inner circle of executives in the company, he'd have to put all his time and energy into work. There'd be nothing left for romance, serious or otherwise.

But all he could think of were Lisa's flashing brown eyes and luscious red mouth.

June settled into a steady routine of preparation for the opening of the inn. The carpenters carpentered, the plasterers plastered, the painters painted. Joe, the general handyman, and his wife Maria, who was in charge of housekeeping, moved next door to Lisa.

Lisa sent letters to the unsuccessful applicants for her job, organized the office, took care of the mail, did the accounts, and sewed. Every drape she hung made her feel that the inn in some small way belonged to her.

One day, when there was a lull in the work and Clinton went about whistling, Lisa got up the nerve to discuss the idea of theme bedrooms for the inn.

She cornered him in the dining room, complete with her folder of sketches.

"You know," she said, "I've been thinking."

"Yes." He gestured for her to sit at one of the tables, then sat down opposite her.

"Well," she said. "Wouldn't it make the inn more interesting if the rooms weren't all alike? We could have some theme rooms. Start out with a couple this year, add three or four more next year."

"Want to explain what you mean by theme rooms?"

"Oh, yes." She pushed the cardboard file into the middle of the table. "The obvious one is a bridal suite. The bed could be heart-shaped, and the curtains have valentine patterns on them. The color scheme would be red and white. Or maybe we could have a few from fairy tales, especially the ones for families with children. You know, one like the interior of a gingerbread cottage. Then there's Winnie-the-Pooh. Or have ones like the mole's or rat's homes from *The Wind in the Willows*, or—''

''Lisa'' Clinton interrupted. ''The rooms are pretty well done. You have the drapes almost finished. What would you do with the drapes you'd have to change?''

Lisa chuckled. ''That's no problem,'' she said. ''We'll save them for the rooms on the second story. Seriously. I said only a couple this year. We can see how they go over and add to them gradually if people like them.''

She shoved the file at him. ''Here are some sketches I made for stage sets of plays I worked on. Most of them are from the last couple of years, but some go back to college and a few to high school days. We might get some ideas from them.''

Clinton grunted and untied the string that kept the cardboard file closed. He carefully shook the sketches out on the table.

''Ah,'' he said, looking at the drawing of a courtroom scene. ''That looks like *The Merchant of Venice*.''

''Yes,'' she said. ''I was Jessica, but I designed the sets too. That was from college.''

''Um.'' He sifted through a few more.

''What's this one?'' He held up a drawing of a woman, done in colored pencils. ''This isn't a stage set.''

Lisa reached for the drawing and blushed. ''Oh, uh, well, I didn't know that was in there.''

''Who is it?''

''Me,'' she said.

Clinton held the picture up in one hand and scrutinized Lisa. ''You? You appear to have dyed your hair, cut six inches from your height, and sold all your clothes. What do you mean, it's you?''

The woman in the picture was tall and willowy, with blond hair and blue eyes. She was dressed in expensive-looking furs. Her fingers were covered with rings. Two stately Russian wolfhounds sat by her side.

"I did that in high school," Lisa said, "when I was sixteen."

"Hmm. Most women gain sophistication with age. You've really gone backward. How about explaining?"

"Well," she said, her face fiery red, "it's not really me. It's Elizabeth Louise. You know, my name's really Elizabeth Louise."

"Yes. I think maybe you've mentioned that. So?"

"Well." She hesitated. "When I was a little girl, I liked to pretend I was a princess. Then when I got older, the fantasies became more specific. I was short and brown and dumpy, and my parents called me Lisa. But the name on my birth certificate was Elizabeth Louise."

She paused and sighed. "Isn't it a lovely name—Elizabeth Louise? I liked to imagine that I matched the name, that I was tall and blond and willowy, and had two dignified wolfhounds named Nicholas and Alexander. And I had jewels and mink coats and all those things instead of jeans and sneakers. Anyway, I outgrew Elizabeth Louise long ago. Actually, that drawing was sort of my farewell to her. I'd forgotten it was in there."

"Hmm. Quite an imagination, haven't you?"

"I guess. Don't you ever pretend you're Mel Gibson?"

He chuckled. "Why should I when I'm so much better-looking?"

"Right," she said. "Of course. Right. Now, what about theme rooms."

Clinton paused and placed the sketches back in a neat pile, put the pile on edge and tapped it for perfect alignment, then turned it ninety degrees and tapped it again. He put the papers back in the folder and retied the string.

Finally he said, ''I'm sorry, Lisa. I don't think so. The rooms are finished and the furniture ordered. Maybe, if we get off to a good start this year, we can think about a couple of rooms for next year, but not now.''

''All right,'' Lisa said. ''It was just an idea.''

The stainless steel commercial kitchen was installed, and the lobby had real furniture and a stone fireplace; the battered desk and filing cabinet disappeared into Clinton's office to join a new computer that matched the one at the reception desk. The brick facing and the landscaping and the pool remained invisible. But the inside things, the essentials, were in place. The motel was ready for business.

The big opening was set for the first week of August. There would be a widely advertised restaurant opening on a Saturday night; then the motel would begin taking reservations for the following weekend, giving the staff another week to get everything shipshape.

Jennifer Masters descended a week before the opening in a swirl of platinum blond hair. She was thin and chic and efficient, lean and mean. She looked as cold as ice. Jennifer was a mature Elizabeth Louise minus the wolfhounds.

Clinton had told the truth. Jennifer was, indeed, the woman in the picture, Clinton's boss, the J of the S and J country inns empire. Watching her, Lisa could understand why she had a chain of very successful inns. It was a bit harder to reconcile her with The Lunenburg Whaler, twenty-five miles from Lunenburg, located between Chester Basin and New Ross, surrounded by Christmas trees and small farms.

Jennifer swept through the place like a blast of arctic air. The housekeeping department was slack; the menus wouldn't do; why on earth hadn't the exterior been finished? She fussed and fumed and replaced the plastic place mats with trendy cotton ones. She ordered fresh flowers for the opening, and haggled with the butcher over cuts of meat.

Jennifer was a tyrant, but for the first time Lisa thought that the inn might really and truly open, that the first night might escape disaster, that there might be a job for a recreation director after all.

The morning of the grand opening, the cook and kitchen staff walked out, demanding better working conditions and more money.

Clinton refused on the grounds that if he gave in now, next week it would be something else. Jennifer agreed. They would manage on their own with Joe and Maria handling the washing up in the kitchen.

The three of them—Clinton and Jennifer and Lisa—sat down at a dining room table and planned their campaign. Jennifer would be in charge of food. Clinton would help her and take care of the money. Lisa would be the waitress.

"Handling a restaurant this size by yourself will be a big job, Lisa," Jennifer said. "Have you ever worked as a waitress?"

Lisa shook her head, then set her mind to thinking about strategies as the rest of the conversation swirled around her.

Clinton set off on errands, and Jennifer turned to Lisa. "Now," she said, "about you—"

"I've been thinking. . . ."

The look on Jennifer's face suggested that the above, on the part of a mere subordinate, might not be a good idea.

Lisa plowed on. "No," she said, "I've never worked as

a waitress. But I could make a map of the tables and number each one. Then I could carry the map on a clipboard, and have a pile of bills clipped on one corner. When I wait on a table, I'll write up the customer's order, then put the table number beside it. After you've dished up the food, if you put the bill beside the plate, I'll know exactly where it goes. I can also give the customer the bill at the same time and save another trip.'' She looked up at Jennifer. ''What do you think?''

''I think,'' Jennifer said, somewhat dryly, ''that in spite of your deplorable lack of experience, there's hope for you yet. Yes. That sounds like a good idea. Now, for some of the other things you'll need to know.''

She taught Lisa the rudiments of being a waitress: modeling the approach to the customer, showing her which side to serve from and which side to clear from.

She couldn't have been more demanding if she'd been directing a Broadway play instead of a lone waitress. Finally, she said, ''I think you'll do. Go take a break until four-thirty. Don't be too hard on yourself. Wear a simple cotton dress or a skirt and top for tonight, with sensible shoes—not sneakers. And big pockets.''

''Big pockets?''

Jennifer sighed. ''You really don't have any experience at this, do you? For your tips, Lisa. For your tips.''

''Oh.'' In all the excitement of being part of a very small team, Lisa hadn't thought about tips. Real money, over and above her modest salary.

''Here,'' Jennifer said, almost as an afterthought, ''why don't you wear my diamond? It might save you some unwanted attention.''

She slipped off the ring and handed it to Lisa. ''Does it fit?''

It fit perfectly.

"It's beautiful," Lisa said, wondering if she would ever wear a ring like this. A fancy flitted across her mind that it was a gift from Clinton rather than a loan from Jennifer. She promptly slapped the fancy down.

Jennifer looked at the huge solitaire on Lisa's left hand. Lisa suspected that Jennifer was childless and fulfilled by her career rather than motherhood.

For the first time Lisa realized that, twenty years from now, she would rather be like her mother Beth than like Jennifer. She would rather have a lovely daughter than a chain of hotels—a daughter much like herself: perhaps a bit taller, perhaps with reddish tints in her dark hair, perhaps with golden flecks in eyes that were more hazel than brown.

Fat chance. The gentleman had made it quite clear he wasn't into marriage. She had made equally clear she wasn't into the kind of marriage he visualized. She might prefer a daughter to a chain of hotels, but that didn't mean she intended to be any man's household pet.

Lisa appeared in the dining room at 4:30, dressed in flat shoes and a simple cotton dress made of a bright floral print in rose and blue and green. It was fresh and cool-looking for the warm summer night.

Jennifer had set the tables with place mats, cutlery, napkins, water glasses, and photocopies of handwritten menus.

Clinton wore a dark suit, a tie, and a shirt so white it dazzled. He looked even better than the imaginary manager of Lisa's fantasy. She glanced at his feet and saw her elongated, skewed reflection in the toes of his black dress shoes. She swallowed and felt compelled to call him Mr. Daniels.

No wonder he'd never pretended he was Mel Gibson. As he'd said, he really was better-looking.

Lisa turned her attention to her map and her stack of bills, doing a paranoid check to see that everything was in place.

The advertising and the low prices had paid off. By 6:00, the restaurant was crowded, and people stood lined up behind a sign that said PLEASE SEAT YOURSELF.

Lisa found that, although from 6:00 to 9:00 she was run off her feet, with Jennifer's coaching and her own map she could cope. There was never a slipup on Jennifer's part. The plates of food were always where they should be, with the bills beside them.

Being friendly and pleasant wasn't a problem. It was easy to smile, to chat, to joke, to flatter the older men, careful to flatter their wives too. These skills came naturally to Lisa.

The last stragglers stopped chatting over drinks and coffee cups shortly after 11:00.

Lisa returned the ring to Jennifer and started picking up dishes.

"Never mind that," Jennifer said. "You and Clinton run along. I've already told Joe and Maria to go. I'll finish up the bit that's left to do here. Sleep in as late as you like. We're not open again until Friday."

Lisa went to her room and emptied her pockets onto the top of her dresser. She whistled to herself. Enough dollar bills to sink the QEII. To say nothing of large numbers of five- and ten-dollar bills, and the occasional twenty. She did a fast count. She could wrest ownership of another month's worth of Pink Sally from the bank.

Maybe she'd missed her calling. Waitressing seemed to pay better than recreation directing ever would.

Physically, she was tired, but emotionally, she was too keyed up to sleep. She needed a breath of outside air. She slipped into jeans and a sweater, then went back through the lobby and out the front doors.

The moon was full. She sat on the steps, knees drawn up and chin in hands, and gazed at it. There were real front steps now. Jennifer had insisted on them for the opening.

The evening had gone very well. Lisa had pulled her weight, and, with Clinton and Jennifer, made up a third of a successful team.

After their chat over breakfast about marriage and Ibsen, Lisa and Clinton had worked together to get the inn ready to open. Tonight had been the culmination. He'd settled into simple friendship. That was just fine with her. She hoped it lasted as long as she stayed at the inn. Of course, she did.

The door creaked behind her, and she jumped to her feet.

Clinton stepped through the doors of the lobby, and together they stood on the landing between the lobby door and the front steps, profiles facing away from each other at right angles.

They both, arms crossed over their chests, looked determinedly at the full moon.

Clinton broke the silence first.

"You know, Lisa," he said, "we're looking at the ocean here. That moon's shining on the ocean, you know."

"Yes," she said, "I know. And my name's Elizabeth Louise. I'm six feet tall, icy blond, and own two Russian wolfhounds. And I wouldn't consider carpentering, sewing, or waitressing when I was hired as a social director."

"Lisa's a much much nicer person than Elizabeth Louise. She does all those things—cheerfully." His voice was low and hypnotic.

He wrapped his arms around her.

She mustn't let herself do this. She must remove herself, right now, she told herself.

"Yes," she murmured, as she leaned against him, surrendering herself to his strength. "And there's something really beautiful about the way a moon shines on a gravel parking lot. Who wants an ocean anyway?"

"My sentiments exactly." He bent his head so that his lips hovered against her hair. He blew into her hair, and she luxuriated in the soft stirring it provoked.

She was on a high, coming down from the successful evening. This moonlit scene, with Clinton nuzzling her hair, holding her in his arms, seemed the perfect conclusion.

Easy friendship and good workmates? She'd worry about that tomorrow.

"Well," he said, after a pause, "it's not likely she'd ever admit it, but I do think my aunt was pleased tonight, don't you?"

Jolted out of her comfortable lethargy, Lisa whirled out of his arms, and turned to face him.

"Your aunt?" she said, then consciously worked to bring her voice down from a screech. "You mean Jennifer's your aunt? You mean that's how you got this job? You mean you don't have to know anything!"

He exhaled audibly. "Yes," he said. "Now you know. You suspected something funny all along, didn't you?"

He gestured toward the building behind them. "A motel that advertises an ocean view, set in the middle of Christmas-tree farms. Landscaping and a pool and tennis courts that are piles of gravel. Hiking trails you'd need a machete and a chain saw to hike on. And the whole thing is run by an unemployed English professor and an unemployed schoolteacher. The inn itself is located a few miles out of Chester and gets its mail from a post office box in Bridgewater, but—it's called The Lunenburg Whaler.

"Would you like to know why it's called The Lunenburg Whaler?"

"I can hardly bear the suspense." She stood looking up at him in the moonlight.

"Because Jennifer's father, also my father's father, was born in Lunenburg. Because there's a legend that his father, her grandfather, my great-grandfather, was a whaling captain. Now, to fit everything else about this outfit, he was probably janitor on a lobster boat. But that's the legend, and that's why Jennifer was set on this motel. The others make money, and they are located to make money. This one is located, mislocated, out of sheer misguided nostalgia. And I think it's intended as a tax write-off. Jennifer would most likely be really upset if it made money, but I don't think she has an immediate problem."

"So why didn't she put this motel in Lunenburg?"

Clinton shrugged. "I suppose all the available land was too expensive."

"I see," was all Lisa could think of to say. She was having trouble adjusting to the thought of Clinton, not as a doomed manager for a doomed motel, but as the heir apparent to the S and J country inns empire. She felt a wave of sympathy for him, being forced by an ambitious family into a career completely foreign to his nature. No wonder he wavered between kind and gentle, and horrid and arrogant.

Clinton went on, "So, you see, if you open a motel out of nostalgia, that's predestined to be a loser anyway, why not make sure of its tax-shelter status and have it managed by an unemployed English professor, and social-directed by an unemployed teacher?''

''Jennifer didn't tell you to hire the unemployed teacher. That was your own idea.''

''I know,'' he said. ''Maybe I haven't completely outgrown my rebel stage.'' He moved his hand up to caress her cheek and her jaw, then let it rest along the side of her neck, stroking her neck, stirring the ends of her short hair.

''Whatever the reasons, that's the thing I've done right,'' he said. ''I can't think of anyone else who would have done, could have done, all the things you did. And tonight—nobody else could have succeeded like you did tonight.''

She rested her head against his hand.

She had done this; she could be a top-notch recreation director too. Clinton had handled the construction crew right, and the kitchen crew, and had managed to get the inn ready by August first. He'd made a pile of rubble into a real motel, and, in the midst of it all, had taken the time to make a cozy room for her.

Clinton was wonderful; she was wonderful; they were both wonderful; this evening had been, still was, wonderful.

She reached up and wound her arms around his neck. ''You aren't giving yourself enough credit,'' she said. ''Think positive. The motel doesn't have to be a loser. We'll show them. We'll show everybody. We'll show your Aunt Jennifer.''

She brought her hands down to his shoulders, shaking him in time to her remarks. ''You're going to be the best manager and I'm going to be the best recreation director, and this motel's going to be the best moneymaker your Aunt Jennifer owns.''

''You tell 'em, Lisa,'' he said. ''Maybe we can at that.

We did tonight.'' He put his arms around her and held her tight. ''You were magnificent, sweetheart,'' he whispered. ''I was so proud of you. Jennifer was proud of you, and she isn't easily pleased.''

Suddenly Lisa realized she was tired with a bone-crushing, overpowering weariness. She yawned into Clinton's shoulder.

It was not the night for Clinton to remember his resolutions about women and getting involved. Lisa was soft and sweet and supportive. Her lovely lips called to his.

He kissed her passionately and, still floating on a high from their recent success, she kissed him back.

He withdrew his mouth, but still held her close against him, his cheek against her hair. He stroked her back, his palm and fingers massaging in sweeping circles. She relaxed against him, her body softly, sweetly, settling into his. In the middle of a tender kiss, her head dropped.

''What . . .'' he said, then realized.

She was sound asleep.

Her arms were still around his neck, but her head slumped onto his shoulder, her cheek turned into him. Her eyes were closed, the long dark lashes lying against her skin, pale in the moonlight. She smelled like garden flowers.

He reached one arm behind her knees and scooped her up. The other arm cradled her against his body. He eased through the main doors without waking her, and carried her across the lobby, to her room. He held her with one arm, while with the other he threw back the duvet and laid her down.

In sleep, she looked sweet and innocent and vulnerable. There would be no real reason later to tell her that he was more than the family charity case. He didn't need Lisa joining a long line of women who, at one time or another, had pursued him for his future expectations.

He removed her shoes. drew the duvet over her, looked down at her a long moment, and tiptoed from the room.

Lisa slept soundly and dreamlessly until near morning. Half-awake, she discovered she was in bed with all her clothes on. Still drowsy, she struggled out of her jeans and sweater. Snuggling back into the duvet, she began to daydream.

She remembered Clinton's kisses. It was just like a scene in a romance novel or in an old movie. She smiled when she remembered what had happened then. She'd yawned. Then—right in the middle of a kiss—she let her head drop onto his shoulder, and she didn't remember anything else until she awakened just now. She'd fallen asleep in his arms.

Then how had she ended up in bed? There was only one possible way. He'd put her there. Now she slept again, to dream again of Clinton.

She awoke at 10:00.

She showered, and dressed in jeans and a red silk shirt. Not that it would be of any use. How did a man react when the woman in his arms fell asleep?

When she reached the lobby, Jennifer met her and hustled her into the dining room.

"Here, dear," she said, "you just sit down. I'll cook pancakes for you. Some fresh strawberries first?"

Lisa suppressed her surprise and said only, "Why, yes. That would be lovely."

She watched Jennifer disappear into the kitchen. The ice queen had thawed.

Clinton appeared with two dishes of fresh strawberries, sprinkled with sugar.

"Jennifer's waiting on us this morning," he said. "Especially on you. She appears to be pleased. I'll be back with your coffee in a minute. Black?"

"Yes. Thank you."

When Clinton appeared with the coffee, he slid into the chair opposite her. They ate strawberries in amicable silence. There were many kinds of silence. There was uncomfortable silence, like the one at the restaurant when Clinton had eaten his Chinese food in a black solitude. This wasn't that kind. This was the comfortable kind of silence, the kind that said, "It's okay. We like each other. We don't have to fill the air with chatter to get along."

His smile was warm and so were the gold lights in his hazel eyes. It was all right. He wasn't angry about the night before. In fact, he seemed to be loving her with his eyes.

Jennifer entered the room. The mood was broken. Conversation turned to business, as Clinton briefed them on his handling of the kitchen strike: he'd hired everyone but the cook back with small raises. The cook had been the ringleader, telling the others that if they all quit, Mr. Daniels would have to offer more money.

"They'll be here on Thursday to get everything ready for customers," Clinton said.

He stretched lazily and placed his hands behind his head, fingers interlocked.

"We've already had a few bookings for the weekend, mainly because of the job we did last night."

Lisa gasped, and raised her hands to her face. "Oh, no!"

Clinton and Jennifer swiveled to stare at her.

"What do you mean, oh, no?" Jennifer asked.

"Regular customers—for the weekend. I'm not ready. I don't have any programs. What am I going to do?"

Clinton must have forgotten the theoretical reason he'd hired her.

"Well," he said, "let's face it, Lisa. People staying in motels are looking for cheap food and clean rooms. They don't want to be entertained."

Jennifer looked at him down her long nose, and Lisa burst out, "Then why did you hire me?"

He shrugged and grinned at her wolfishly. "Because you had a nice nose and cute freckles."

Even though I don't know anything. She slammed her coffee cup down on the table, and stormed out.

Chapter Five

Lisa stomped into her office, slamming the door behind her. She'd show Clinton Daniels. She'd just show him. He'd see how much difference she could make. He'd see when she got tons and tons of return bookings.

She remembered the fight at the Chinese restaurant and the little chat over breakfast the next morning. He didn't take her seriously. She had just as much education as he had, but he was a man, so he was manager. She was a woman, so she typed and sorted the mail and did the dog work on the books.

"Me, Tarzan; you, Jane. Me hunt tigers; you sweep cave." Not!

She had an urge to hurl the sewing machine, the ledger, and the laptop straight through the window, but instead she put away the sewing machine, switched on the computer, and threw herself into a frenzy of activity.

Real customers, ones staying for the whole weekend,

were arriving in a week, and she had nothing ready. She pulled out the index cards and file folders she'd so optimistically carted down here over two months ago. She found the books she'd forgotten to return to the public library.

Ideas shot through her head: combinations of things she'd learned from her education courses, things she remembered from her own days in recreation programs, things from books, and things from her imagination.

She'd show him, she told herself through clenched teeth. She'd show him. Nice nose and cute freckles indeed.

For the next week, she worked nonstop, churning out the plans: mixers, noisy games, quiet games, indoor games, outdoor games.

She badgered Joe until he put real horseshoe pits in the middle of the imaginary swimming pool, and she bought horseshoes in Bridgewater.

Later, if not for this year then for next, she'd arrange for chartered bus tours to Lunenburg, Yarmouth, and the Annapolis Valley. She pushed aside the little voice reminding her that this motel might never open for the next season and that if it did it might very well open without a social and recreation director.

Through it all, she typed Clinton's letters and did Clinton's bookkeeping and took care of Clinton's mail.

The guests who arrived on Friday included several retired couples from the United States, some anniversary and birthday celebrants, and one couple on their honeymoon.

Promptly at 4:00 on Friday afternoon, dressed in her fuchsia interview suit and armed with name tags, Lisa swung into action. She would be a recreation director who didn't have to take a backseat to any graduate of a tourism or recreation program.

She introduced herself to all the guests, chatting with them, asking them about themselves, and telling them to go to the dining room at 4:30.

Clinton frowned as she charged by him.

"Lisa."

She stopped so fast that she slid the last two feet. "Yes?"

"Don't you think you're overdoing things a bit? Being friendly is one thing, but harassing people is another."

She paused, hands on hips, and snarled. "What would you know about it?" she said. "Your idea of a motel is clean sheets and rare roast beef with gallons of gravy."

"Lisa, I probably know more about it than you do. I have, after all, been in the hotel business for longer than you have."

"Right," she said. "A month or two longer." Then she hurried on her way.

So, she'd done it again. Would she never learn to control her mouth? The man was her boss.

What would have happened if she'd talked to her principal that way? But her principal had been a reasonable person. Her principal had never interfered with the way she did her job. Her principal had never affected her pulse rate every time he looked at her.

She stopped and took several deep breaths to calm herself before continuing on her way.

"Now," she said to the guests assembled in the dining room at 4:30, "I've met most of you, and, as you know, I'm Elizabeth Louise Bannerman, your recreation and social director, but why don't you just call me Lisa?"

She added, "And now, you're going to get acquainted

with one another. I've got name cards for you all. Come get yours when I call your name and then pin it on where everybody can see it."

"There," she said, when everybody sported a plastic-encased name card, "you've already seen who everyone is. Now we're going to play a game to break the ice. Everybody line up in alphabetical order."

The guests scurried around and checked name cards as Lisa had intended. Finally, a row of about thirty people stood in a straggling line. *There. Take that, Clinton Daniels.* So he thought she couldn't handle the position of social director, did he?

She walked down the row and tapped every second person. "Now," she said, "the people I've tapped are to take two steps to the left so we'll have two lines. Good. Now just stay there for a moment."

When they stood obediently, Lisa disappeared into the kitchen and returned with two grapefruits. Oblivious to the groans, she persisted. "The purpose of this game is to pass the grapefruit down the row by your necks and chins. You aren't allowed to touch it with your hands. If it drops you have to move it back two people. When it reaches the end, the last person runs to the front with it. Got it?"

She looked at Clinton. If he thought he was going to stand around in his dark suit and shiny shoes and look superior and criticize, he had another think coming.

"Here, Mr. Daniels. You have to play too. Just get yourself into row two, between Cameron and Foster." She gave him a little push.

"Lisa," he growled into her ear, "I'm going to get you for this."

"Now, now, Mr. Daniels, we do all have to be good sports, don't we?" As she moved to the front of a line, she said, "Everybody in the winning row gets a ticket for free dessert."

She helped the American gentleman at the head of the other row secure his grapefruit under his chins; then she secured her own, and, in a somewhat strangled voice, yelled, "Go!"

Five minutes later amid squashed grapefruit and flying juice a winner was declared, and Lisa handed out the tickets.

"I think *anybody* who took part in that fiasco deserves free dessert," Clinton muttered through his teeth, as he wiped grapefruit pulp from his tie and jacket.

"Okay. Hey, folks, hey, just a minute." She clapped her raised hands frantically and called after the guests who stampeded through the doors to wash up for dinner. "Hey, come back a minute. Now," she said, all breathless from shouting, "our manager has generously said that because this is our first full weekend, he'd like to give everybody free dessert, so if the rest of you would come collect your tickets—

"And if the ladies will just leave your name cards with me, then when you come back for dinner, the gentlemen will draw them out of a box for dinner partners."

The guests raced for the door. Only Clinton lingered, standing three feet away and breathing fire.

"I am going to get you for this, Lisa. I really am. And I didn't say I was giving free desserts because it was opening weekend. You heard me quite clearly. I said I was pacifying them for having been subjected to the grapefruit game."

Shortly before dinner, Lisa stood by the dining room door, supervising the draw for partners.

The free desserts pacified everyone but the honeymoon-ers, Harvey and Elaine. Elaine sat and listened to a retired American talk to her about fishing from Texas to Alaska, while Harvey stared glumly at the English spinster who carried her knitting with her everywhere, even to the dining-room table.

Lisa stood up again, right after dessert, before anyone could escape.

"I hope you had a nice dinner," she said. "Enjoy your coffee. This evening I'm going to teach you all to play that traditional Nova Scotia card game, 45s."

"What's wrong with bridge?" muttered a blue-haired lady from New York.

"What's wrong with blackjack?" muttered her dinner partner, a retired gentleman from Las Vegas.

"What's wrong with going to bed early?" muttered Harvey. Elaine, from across the room, caught his eye and winked.

"We'll all meet back here in thirty minutes," continued Lisa, as if she hadn't heard the simmering rebellion.

She stood at the door, smiling at everyone who left. Harvey, his hand protectively on Elaine's back, stopped. "Oh, Miss," he said, "I hate to skip the rest of the fun, but I don't think we'll be coming back. My wife has a slight headache, so if you'd just excuse us from the cards."

They couldn't. They just couldn't. If people started leaving, her whole program would collapse. And after all the work she'd put into preparing it . . .

Even if they were honeymooners, surely Harvey and Elaine could spend an hour or two learning 45s. She had to prove to Clinton and Jennifer that she could run a successful program, especially now that she had to atone for the grapefruit game.

"Why don't I just get an aspirin for her?" she said aloud.

Elaine smiled a little smile that was almost a smirk.

"Uh, um, well," Harvey mumbled, "that's very nice of you, but I don't think so."

Lisa was about to protest further, but suddenly Clinton was at her side.

"Lisa," Clinton said, "could I speak to you for a minute?" He drew her out of the doorway to the side of the room while Harvey and Elaine made their escape.

"I think things are going just marvelously, don't you?" Lisa bubbled as she leaned against the wall, Clinton looming over her, one hand propped above her head.

She couldn't. Even Lisa, with her incurable optimism, could not possibly think things were going well. She was just stubborn and pigheaded.

"Well, actually," he said, "that's what I wanted to talk to you about."

"What do you mean?"

"Lisa. Unless it's a singles club where people come to meet people, drawing partners for dinner isn't a good idea. Then there's Harvey and Elaine."

"Yes?"

"I don't think they're interested in passing grapefruits under chins, or in learning to play 45s. Harvey and Elaine are on their honeymoon."

"But—"

His eyes were drawn to Lisa's lips, ripe and luscious. After the little chat at breakfast, weeks ago, he'd resolved to keep his distance. True, he'd told her not to get ideas, but keeping himself from getting them was not so easy. He'd succeeded until last Saturday night. On Sunday, after strawberries, he'd made the resolution all over again. Now he found himself once more breaking down.

He brought his free hand up to her face and caressed it.

She turned away. "It's time to set up for 45s," she said.

The evening that had started so badly went steadily downhill. Harvey and Elaine weren't the only ones to stay away, and many of the others appeared to have come because they didn't want to hurt Lisa's feelings rather than because they wanted to play cards.

She tried to be friendly and enthusiastic, but so many guests excused themselves early that she had to give up before 9:00.

When the last guest left, Lisa bolted for the doors. Clinton followed her to the lobby, and reached out to stop her as she tried to circle past him.

He was annoyed with her for knowing so little about the job she was trying to do; he was annoyed with himself for having hired her. Above all, he rebuked himself for being attracted to her.

But tonight Lisa was hurting. She'd knocked herself out trying to make his inn a success, and it had backfired. This was neither the time to discuss her shortcomings with her nor to ignore her.

He would be friendly and supportive. His comfort would be the warm comfort of a friend. Nothing more.

"So what are you planning next?" he asked. Some resident demon compelled him to run one hand up and down the sleeve of her fuchsia suit.

"Going to bed, I guess. It's been a long and tiring day."

"And once you're in bed, you're going to drop right off into a sound and dreamless sleep?"

She concentrated on peeling long strips of fuchsia polish from her thumbnail, then stopped.

"Sorry," she said. "Thought I'd given up this habit in eleventh grade."

She took a deep breath and looked up. "No, I won't sleep. I'm going to toss and turn and think about everything I did wrong. Oh, Clinton, it was awful. I'm sorry."

"It's okay," he said. He placed his hand on her back and moved it up and down. "You blew it. I'd be lying if I said anything else. But we all blow it sometimes. I don't think there's anything to gain by your tossing and turning all night, flagellating yourself. Go to your room and change into something casual, and meet me in the lobby?"

She nodded, sniffled, and left.

Clinton went to his own apartment and changed, throwing his shirt and pants to join the grapefruit-stained jacket and tie already in a heap for dry-cleaning. He dressed in jeans and a comfortable sweatshirt, then returned to the lobby and waited for Lisa, pacing up and down, reminding himself the comfort he would give her would be the comfort of a friend.

"Come on," he said when she came back to the lobby in jeans and sweater. "Let's go for a walk."

He reached for her hand and led her down the front steps.

"Where are we going?"

He shrugged. "Where do you want to go? Maybe we could have a swim or play a round of tennis. Or what about a walk on one of our many hiking trails?"

She didn't even smile.

"Or maybe we could just mosey down the highway a bit." He put an arm around her shoulders.

"Oh, Clinton." She shrunk against him. "It was awful. I'm just awful. I'm no more a social director than, than . . ." She paused and sniveled again, then finished, "Than the swimming pool's a swimming pool."

Very true, but it didn't seem diplomatic to agree with her at the moment.

Instead he squeezed her shoulder.

"Come on, Lisa."

He held her tight against him as they strolled down the driveway, along the highway, and back. The same moon was shining as had shone the week before, but the magic had gone.

"I'm cold," she said, shivering against him.

"Okay. We'll go in. But you're not going off to bed to worry all night."

Tomorrow he'd have to talk to her seriously, make some suggestions, emphasize that her future with the inn depended on her making some changes.

He took her to the lobby and sat her down on the sofa while he built a fire.

"Stay there," he ordered and left. When he came back, he carried a tray with two mugs of hot chocolate, topped with sugar-sweet whipped cream.

He placed the tray on the coffee table, then turned out all the lights before he sat down by Lisa. Only the flames from the fireplace lighted the large lobby.

"Here," he said, handing Lisa a mug, then picking up his own. "Drink this."

Lisa licked at the whipped cream, then began to sip the hot chocolate. "It's good."

She looked solemnly over the rim at Clinton as she drank. When she finished, she set the mug back on the tray. "Thank you," she said.

He put down his own mug, then touched her upper lip. "You've got a whipped-cream moustache," he said, then watched enchanted as she put out her tongue and tucked her top lip under so that she could lick off the last of the cream. How could he possibly stick to his good intentions?

He moved his lips onto hers, tasting whipped cream and chocolate. Looking into her eyes, he said, "You're a very delicious person, you know. I was going to tell you that last week over strawberries, but Jennifer interrupted."

They heard footsteps entering the lobby and passing on through.

"Just relax," Clinton said. "It's only Jennifer going to her room."

"What if she saw us kissing?"

Clinton's mouth curved into a lazy grin. "How old are you, Lisa?"

"Twent—" she started to answer him, then broke off. "You know very well how old I am."

"There," he said, "that's better. You're twenty-six, and I'm twenty-nine. What I'm trying to say is, what difference does it make whether or not she saw us? We're of age. She's of age. And what we were doing wouldn't cause raised eyebrows in a PG movie. So let's forget Jennifer and treasure the moment."

"But—" Lisa protested.

"You didn't like it?"

"Oh," was all she could manage.

"That's my Lisa," he replied.

"Oh, Clinton," she said. "What if Jennifer fires me?"

"Hey," he said, "I just told you—"

"Oh, not for that. For being so incompetent tonight."

"Jennifer doesn't have the authority to fire you," he said. "She can make recommendations, but when push comes to shove, I'm the one who does the firing."

"I don't want to be fired by either of you. And then, I

have to run a program again tomorrow night. What will I do?''

''Okay,'' he said, we'll talk. Now what do you think went wrong tonight? What parts of the program itself were unsuitable?''

''The grapefruit game,'' she said.

''Absolutely. The grapefruit game. When nobody in the whole world likes it, it's a mystery to me why social directors keep using it. Why *did* you use it?''

''Well, it was a mixer. It was meant to break the ice and have people get to know one another.''

''Okay. So why don't you look through all those index cards of yours and find a way of breaking the ice that won't be quite so hard on clothes? Now, what about your way of finding dinner partners?''

Lisa remembered Harvey and Elaine. ''I guess some people want to eat dinner with the partners they brought with them.''

''I think that's true. But I also think people do want to make new friends. So why don't you leave the mixers and fun and games voluntary, instead of forcing people to play? For dinner partners, why don't you keep the same system, but only for the people who choose to, and why don't you let them turn in their name tags in pairs if they want, so that couples can meet other couples. Get the idea?''

''But—''

''Yes?''

''It's my job as social director to think of things for people to do.''

''Correction. It's your job as social director to make the inn a place where people can enjoy themselves. Making them play the messy grapefruit game and then forcing your idea of an evening activity on them isn't exactly helping them enjoy themselves. This isn't a classroom, where everybody does as you say, no questions asked.''

She looked about to protest, then paused. "Yes. You're right. I guess I can come up with something to redeem myself by tomorrow evening.''

He tightened his arm around her. "It wasn't all bad, Lisa. You made a good impression on a lot of people. Your enthusiasm is great. And your basic ideas were good. Just don't push it down their throats.''

She sighed. "There's still Jennifer.''

"What about her?''

"Do you think she's just going to ignore this whole fiasco? Oh, no. I still have to face Jennifer in the morning.''

"Didn't I just make clear who does the firing? But if Jennifer wants to discuss your performance, don't get your back up. Jennifer's one competent lady. She's worth listening to.''

"All right. I'll listen. I'll pay attention to her advice.''

She added, "It's okay. Really it is. I'll handle it.'' She stood up and bent over him, touching her soft lips against his.

"Thanks.'' She turned from him and walked down the long hall toward her room.

Clinton returned the mugs to the kitchen. He was terribly afraid he was falling in love with Lisa. Ignoring her didn't work. Friendship didn't work. He was in no position to offer commitment, but he was incapable of leaving her alone.

When she'd gone to bed, Lisa had turned the problem of how to handle Jennifer over to her subconscious, confident that in the morning she'd wake up with a clear idea of what to do.

The cheerful confidence was dispelled by the morning sun. It was all very well to feel optimistic when she went to bed, warmed by Clinton's kisses, but in the cold light of day as she sat sipping coffee and nibbling on a piece of toast, Lisa's doubts came back. Did Clinton feel the same way she did, or had he just felt sorry for her? Were the hot chocolate and the kissing just the adult equivalent of the way her mother used to bring her cocoa and then rub her back when she'd hurt herself or had a quarrel with a friend when she was a child?

She didn't want Clinton's sympathy. She wanted more. She remembered his expressed views on love and commitment, and then she remembered Jennifer.

When Jennifer walked by her, looking down her nose, and said, "Could I see you in my office, Lisa?", the cold lump in the pit of her stomach was almost as heavy as it had been the previous night when the last guest left the dining room.

Sure, Clinton had assured her that he did the firing, but she didn't want to hang onto her job because the manager had a soft spot for a nice nose and cute dimples.

She quickly swallowed the rest of her coffee, leaving the remnants of cold toast on the plate; then she followed Jennifer through the lobby and down the hall to her office. Lisa shifted from one foot to the other, while Jennifer, in a full denim skirt and crisp white blouse, sat behind her desk.

Lisa wasn't sure whether the fact Jennifer didn't gesture for her to sit down was oversight or intentional, but she wasn't taking a chance. She stood where she was, gazing at a spot over Jennifer's left shoulder.

Jennifer opened abruptly. "You don't have any qualifications for this job, do you, Lisa?"

"Well," Lisa defended herself, "I'm enthusiastic and I'm a hard worker."

"Yes," Jennifer agreed, "I know that. You made that very obvious the night of the opening. I was pleased and grateful. But businesses don't operate on gratitude. I wasn't quite so pleased last night. Do you have any idea why Clinton hired you?"

"No," Lisa admitted. "I guess I've wondered that. Maybe there weren't any other applications." She remembered the tourism types. Maybe Jennifer didn't know about them.

But Jennifer knew. "Yes, there were. I've been through the personnel files. There were several applicants who had degrees in tourism and fine references."

"Well, then, I don't know. Maybe he liked my enthusiasm." She remembered the interview, but she didn't think describing it to Jennifer would help her to hold on to her job.

"Last night your enthusiasm seemed your main problem," Jennifer commented dryly. "Do you want to know why I think he hired you?"

Suddenly Lisa didn't want to know, but she could hardly say that. Her reluctant "Why?" was little above a whisper.

"I think he was playing one-upmanship with me. He hadn't wanted to run this inn to begin with. Also, he and I don't see eye to eye on the central function of recreation directors in each of our inns. He thinks that position can be filled after the inn's up and running—if at all. I feel the recreation director must be part of the team from the very beginning. I think he hired you just to show me. Figuratively speaking, he was sticking out his tongue and saying, 'So there, Aunt Jennifer. I've hired your recreation director like you wanted.' "

What had Clinton said that night of the opening? That he'd hired her because he hadn't completely outgrown his rebel stage? Right now wasn't the time to think about that. Right now, she had to worry about keeping her job.

She took a deep breath and concentrated on pacifying Jennifer.

"Look, Ms. Masters," she said, finally establishing eye contact, "I'm sorry. I really am. I know I blew it last night. Clinton and I had a long talk about it afterward. We discussed what I did wrong, and we came up with some strategies for improving things. Would you like to hear them?"

"No," Jennifer said, "I don't think so. It will soon be obvious how your strategies are working. I'd suggest that you forget about entertaining people for the rest of this week, think things through, and try again next Friday."

She paused and added, "Good luck, Lisa."

"Thanks," Lisa said as she turned to go.

"By the way," Jennifer said, and Lisa turned back to her, "speaking of Clinton, I couldn't care less how the two of you spend your free time as long as you do a good job of running the inn. But it might be fair to tell you that Clinton has no intention of getting serious for years. If you have some idea he might marry you, you might as well forget it. If you allow yourself to get emotionally involved, you'll just get hurt."

"I have no intention of getting emotionally involved," Lisa said somewhat stiffly.

"And," Jennifer added, "if you're considering him your ticket to riches via the S and J Corporation, forget that too. You wouldn't be the first to try."

Lisa yelped. "What! How da—" She remembered she was here to hold on to her job.

But the very idea was so preposterous. "Riches!" she

said. "But Clinton's not rich. What do you mean? I know you gave him this job, but it's just a crummy little motel in the middle of nowhere." She mentally kicked herself. Would she never stop letting her mouth outrun her brain?

"Sorry," she added. "I shouldn't have said that. But you must think I'm really poor if I consider one old beat-up station wagon evidence of riches. And I know he wears a suit in front of the public, but the clothes he wears the rest of the time don't look like they exactly cost a fortune."

Jennifer smiled a wintry smile. "Sit down, Lisa," she said. "You seem to be operating on incomplete information. At least you've reassured me on the fortune-hunting bit. Unless, of course, you're lying."

The nerve of the woman. Lisa opened her mouth to retort, then closed it again and perched on the corner of the wooden chair in front of Jennifer's desk.

"Lisa," Jennifer said, "Clinton is not just the manager of the Lunenburg Whaler. He's the company trouble-shooter. We send him out to get unprofitable inns on their feet. And to get new inns up and running. He's very good at what he does. Eventually we want him back in the head office as part of the team with his father and myself and Silas, but first I want him to have a wide and varied experience."

"But—the station wagon—"

"Clinton thinks, and I agree, that if you're dealing with the employees of struggling country inns flaunting money doesn't help. He feels that he gets along better with people if he fits in." She smiled again, with more warmth. "However, you needn't worry about him being poverty-stricken. He owns a Jaguar he leaves in Toronto and makes a six-figure salary—not a minimum six figures, either."

"I see," Lisa muttered and stumbled to her feet. "Why didn't he tell me?"

"Well," Jennifer said, "I suppose if you don't want your employees to think you're wealthy, you don't really explain the situation to them, do you? I'd suggest that you not tell Clinton that I've given you this information. And whatever you do, don't share it with anyone else."

Lisa turned and hurled herself out the door. The nerve. Accusing her of falling in love with Clinton. Accusing her of being a fortune hunter.

Worst of all, at the very end reminding her that she was a humble employee like all the rest of them. Reminding her that Clinton felt the same way.

All right. If Clinton saw her simply as an employee, that's what she'd be. No more games on the side. Obviously, that's what it was to Clinton—just a game.

Her face burned with embarrassment. How Clinton must have laughed to himself when she'd wrapped her arms around his neck and told him he was going to be the best manager his Aunt Jennifer had. She'd see that he didn't have any chances to laugh at her again.

Hands off, as far as Clinton Daniels was concerned. She'd be an employee only, professional and aloof.

The knowledge of Clinton's true position in the company came as a shock to say the least. First, she'd wondered how he'd gotten this job. Next, she'd assumed he was a beneficiary of nepotism.

She remembered how he handled the carpenters' wildcat strike and the kitchen walkout. She should have been suspicious then. Clinton wasn't the unemployed professor-turned-motel manager she'd assumed.

Maybe in her year and a half of teaching, the people

skills she'd prided herself on had degenerated until they weren't that great for understanding anyone over nineteen.

Clinton blocked her way as she stormed down the hall to the lobby.

"So, did you survive?" he asked.

He looked almost as if he cared.

"Yes," she said coolly as she stopped, "I've survived."

He touched her arm. "So what's the matter? Why the icy reception? Did something go wrong?"

"Go wrong?" she asked. "Oh, no. Nothing went wrong. Nothing at all."

"You aren't acting as if nothing went wrong," he challenged.

She wasn't about to repeat everything Jennifer had said, but she could probably share the beginning part of it, especially since he'd already admitted it.

"Jennifer told me you'd hired me just to spite her," she said, looking him straight in the face. "Is that true?"

"Well, uh," he said, "I guess there are levels of truth."

He took her by the arm and steered her toward a sofa and sat down with her. She pulled her arm away and scuttled to the other end of the sofa.

"It's not really a lie, but on the other hand, it wasn't really spite either," he told her. "Jennifer had insisted I hire a social and recreation director."

"Huh," she said. "I thought you were in sole charge of hiring and firing."

"I am," he said. "But Jennifer's a very smart lady, and also pleasing her is my fast track to Toronto and a better job. Now, Lisa, you remember what this place looked like the first day?"

She bit back her anger and nodded.

"In your wildest imagination, was there any possible use for a social and recreation director?"

She shook her head.

"Now, I didn't see why I couldn't technically go along with Jennifer, and still forward my own agenda. What I needed was a typist, a bookkeeper, a seamstress. I needed somebody to hold Sheetrock. And scrub floors and wash windows if it should become necessary, although I hoped it wouldn't—and it didn't.

"I hoped somebody who would apply for a job so out of her field might be willing to do all those things. What tipped the scale," he added, grinning, "was the fact that you could type sixty words a minute, and owned your own laptop. I was totally honest about hiring you because you could type and sew wasn't I?"

"Of course," she said.

What a shame the grapefruit that spattered his coat and tie hadn't been rotten!

Chapter Six

I'm not going to make the same mistakes tonight, Lisa vowed as she greeted incoming guests on the following Friday afternoon. Remembering Jennifer's advice, she added, *and I'm not going to make the same mistakes after the program either.*

After all, it wasn't just Jennifer. Hadn't Clinton himself warned her? *"A couple of kisses are not a proposal of marriage."* How could she have forgotten so quickly and have allowed herself to become emotionally involved? Clinton wasn't just another casual date. If she wasn't going to get hurt—more hurt than she already was—she had to stay out of his arms.

The idea that anybody could possibly consider her a gold digger! Was that what she'd be labeled if she got too friendly with Clinton?

If only he were just an unemployed professor who'd

been lucky enough to find a job as a motel manager—the way she'd thought at first.

The firm's troubleshooter? The heir and a future CEO of S & J?

She'd better behave in such a way that nobody could possibly accuse her of chasing him for money or any other reason.

During the past week, she'd managed to keep her behavior around him cordial but professional. On this, her second Friday night as a social director, she intended to redeem herself for last weekend.

"Hi," she said to each guest, "I'm Lisa, your social director. If you'd like to meet your fellow guests and play some games to get acquainted, come to the dining room at four-thirty."

Most of the guests came. She chatted with them as she pinned on name tags.

"Now," she said, "you all have name tags. You have thirty minutes to discover three things about each person in the room—such things as occupation, hobbies, children.

"We'll serve free dessert to those of you who get three pieces of information about at least ten people."

She handed out paper and pencils and said, "Go!" and stood back and watched.

It worked; there was none of the thinly veiled resentment of the grapefruit game. After half an hour she called "Time," and gave instructions for those who wanted to draw for dinner partners. During dinner, when Lisa table-hopped and visited, she found her guests were having a good time.

After dinner she said, "The official activity for this evening is line dancing. I'll demonstrate the steps before we start. If you don't care for line dancing, there are cards and tables and magazines in the lobby.''

That night Lisa went to bed, not in humiliation, but with the cheerful echoes of country and western music ringing in her ears.

The inn was off to a successful start. The food was good; the prices were reasonable. The evaluation forms handed in at the end of each evening showed Lisa that her program was a success.

When she had free time between typing and bookkeeping and entertaining guests, she cleared hiking trails through the woods. These trails were important to her. Her favorite childhood memories included those of her dad taking her for walks and teaching her the names of all the plants and birds and animals. Lisa determined to share her love of nature with the children who visited the inn.

For trail cutting, she used neither a machete nor a chain saw, but rather a Boy Scout hatchet and a brush whip.

She was out on Wednesday afternoon, the third week of August, a blue-and-gold day which brought with it anticipation of the first days of autumn.

She whacked away at an oak about four inches thick at the base. Sweat ran down the back of her neck, and, although the worst of the bug season was over, she had to swat the occasional horsefly.

''Here.'' Clinton's voice came from behind her. When she turned around, there he stood, chain saw in one hand and yellow hard hat in the other. Her breath came faster and her heart beat harder just looking at him. She gave him a cool glance.

He held the hat out to her.

''Hello, Clinton,'' she said. ''Thank you for bringing me

the hat, but I don't really need it. I'm not cutting anything very large.''

''That tree you're on,'' he reminded her, ''is twice as thick as a baseball bat and much longer. Put the hat on.''

''Tyrant,'' she muttered under her breath. She laid down the hatchet, took the hat and fitted it on her head.

''Very fetching.''

''You came out here to bring me a hard hat?''

''Yes.''

''Why?''

He chuckled. ''So if you kill yourself you can't sue me for having you work in unsafe conditions. But mostly I came out here to ask you what's been going on for the last week and a half.''

''What do you mean?'' she asked, hedging.

''You know very well what I mean, and don't try to tell me you're upset because you found out why I hired you. You knew that all along. Friday night a week ago was as torrid as a rain forest, and by Saturday a deep freeze set in and still hasn't thawed. Did you decide that Friday night was a mistake?''

Oh! Torrid as a rain forest. As if she were the one who'd started it.

''Yes,'' she said. ''I've probably decided that.''

He propped himself with one hand against a tree. ''Why? Can't you trust yourself?''

''Of course I can, and right now I'm proving it. I think the fun and games have gone on long enough. You are the manager of this inn. I am the social director, and that's all. I think it's time we both remembered that.''

''So what brought on this momentous decision?''

Lisa drew herself up stiffly. ''I've decided that considering we've agreed neither of us is ready to get serious, maybe we should just cool things a bit.''

''And what,'' he said, ''makes you think neither of us is ready to get serious, and why did you choose this week to get so uptight about it?''

Lisa stood and glared at him.

There was no way she'd admit to him Jennifer had as much as accused her of being after his future money. Never mind the fact that he'd been lying to her about himself from the very beginning.

He let go of the tree and stepped toward her. ''Lisa,'' he said. ''Talk. Now.''

''All right,'' she said, hands on hips. ''Jennifer told me you weren't about to get serious, and that if I kept, uh, seeing you, I'd just get hurt.'' She couldn't bring herself to say ''emotionally involved.'' Everybody knew what ''emotionally involved'' meant. She couldn't admit that to Clinton.

When she saw the flicker of amusement in his eyes, she realized he also knew what ''uh, seeing you,'' meant. She glowered at him again. ''And,'' she added, ''just in case you've forgotten, you told me the same thing at the very beginning, and I agreed with you. We'd agreed to be just friends, but that didn't seem to be working.''

He started to run his hand through his hair, only to come up against the rim of the hard hat. Instead, he scratched his hairline with his thumbnail, and grinned down at Lisa.

''Look, Lisa,'' he said, ''I know I told you that. I think perhaps a man has a right to change his mind. However, a man also has to change his circumstances, and while the mind might have changed, the circumstances unfortunately have not.''

"Oh, really. How considerate of you to share that with me."

These "circumstances" were another excuse, obviously, to keep her on the hook without getting serious. He didn't know that Jennifer had already blown the whistle on his "poverty-stricken young man trying desperately to get ahead" persona.

"Perhaps," she said, "we should postpone this conversation then until that happens. For now, Mr. Daniels, may I just go back to my work?"

Clinton looked down at her feet. "You're wearing sneakers!"

"Of course," she said. "I always wear sneakers."

"Not in my employ you don't. Using an ax with sneakers! Just get out of my way and drag brush to the side of the trail."

He stepped back, picked up the chain saw, and pulled the rope to start it. Lisa watched as the tree she'd sweated over with little beaver chips fell in a few seconds. He cut it up, then moved on up the trail, cutting out brush and small trees. She moved behind him dragging the brush into heaps.

At the end of the trail was a pond she hadn't known existed, a pond with cattails and reeds, and, in a far corner, a beaver house. All around the banks grew pine trees and white birch.

"Look," she said to Clinton. "A lake."

"It's a pond," he said. "It's probably about three feet deep at most." He turned off the chain saw, and stood by her, looking at the serene beauty of the water.

She looked at the heaps by the side of the path. "What will we do with this brush?" she asked.

"Put it beside the swimming pool," he said. "Then in

the evenings we can drag it down bit by bit, and the kids can roast wieners and marshmallows.''

''That's where I have the horseshoe pits.''

''Put the bonfires to one side. It's a big swimming pool. There's room for everyone.''

He set the chain saw on the ground. ''That's enough for today.'' He removed his own hard hat and placed it on top of the chain saw. ''Come here.''

''What do you mean, come here?''

''I mean, come here. I've explained my previous behavior and my change of heart. Now come here.''

She looked at him. She hesitated. She remembered his driving her around Bridgewater until her room was ready. She remembered how he had comforted her that Friday night everything went wrong. She'd suspected she might be falling in love with him. In the last ten days, angry and humiliated as she'd been, she'd had no reason to change her mind about that.

She knew he didn't share her feelings; there was no reason to change her mind about that either.

''Forget it,'' she said.

He stepped toward her, standing so close she could smell sweat and chain-saw oil. She drew back and looked up into his face. Longing overcame common sense. She traced with a finger the groove made in his forehead by the hard hat.

He reached out with one hand and cupped her chin. His touch sent her blood tingling, racing. She threw caution to the winds and fell into his arms. Suddenly, his mouth was on hers and her mouth was on his.

You've just proved that you're a stupid little fool, she said to herself, when they paused for breath.

The next day, when Lisa came to lunch, she discovered a gift-wrapped box beside her plate. Curious, she opened it, to find a pair of steel-toed construction boots in her size.

She chuckled and went to her room, changing into panty hose and the fuchsia suit, then putting on the construction boots. She deliberated a moment before adding the yellow hard hat.

She moved down the hall and tapped on the door of Clinton's office.

"It's open," he said.

She stepped inside. "Hi, Boss. Reporting for work." She struck a suitable pose. "Do you find me suitably dressed today?" She held her arms up and snapped her fingers, kicked a leg out like a dancer, and said, "Tah-da."

"Hold it. Just like that." He opened a desk drawer and drew out a Polaroid camera. He snapped a picture of her, and pinned it on the bulletin board behind him.

"Now," he growled, "come here," and he stood and held out his arms. "You don't need the hard hat," he added. "This is not a high-risk activity."

"You're right," she said. "That's because there isn't going to be any kind of activity at all. I think my point was well proved yesterday. I don't need any more of your little speeches about how this will never happen again—at least not until you have another chance. So, hands off, Clinton. As you said, this will never happen again."

He shrugged. "Maybe you're right," he said. "All right. Friends."

He placed one arm around her shoulders, swung her toward the bulletin board, and chuckled. "In the meantime, I now have my favorite pinup with me all the time."

The picture had finished developing, and Lisa was caught for eternity, one foot kicked out before her, hands up and out, in the act of posing, snapping her fingers, saying, "Tah-da."

The days rolled onward. The job proceeded nicely—the relationship with Clinton, not so well.

She'd certainly made several kinds of fool of herself that day on the trail when he'd brought her the hard hat. The next day in his office when she posed in the construction boots, she'd slapped down his advances, but had she slapped down her own feelings?

Were these feelings love? The feelings that made her crumple every time he touched her, smiled at her? Of course not.

Jennifer had warned her that nothing could ever come of any romantic entanglement. He'd warned her of the same thing himself. Not only that, he'd lied about the reason. He couldn't get serious until he'd established himself financially, he'd said. If the firm's number one troubleshooter with a six-figure salary wasn't established financially, she wasn't sure who would be. Unless he assumed that her expectations rivaled those of Catherine the Great.

Lately, Jennifer seemed to have warmed toward her and no longer looked at her as if she were stealing the family farm every time she came near Clinton. That was the relationship she had to keep her sights on—the one where Jennifer approved of her professional attitude. That, and an objective one with Clinton. She didn't want to end up in an entanglement which would result in his having to fire her or her having to quit.

When the first of the trails was complete, on Saturday and Sunday afternoons she led groups of hikers over it and taught them about the plants, the trees, the flowers, the mosses, and the birds of the area. The retired men began to gather at the horseshoe pits while their wives played cards or drove into Chester.

It was what she'd hoped for. The inn was holding its own, and she was confident much of the credit belonged to her. True, it was not yet making money, but Jennifer seemed pleased that it came close to breaking even.

One evening, after the activities were over and the guests retired to their rooms, the three of them sat in front of the big fireplace in the lobby. Jennifer said to Clinton and Lisa, ''You two are doing so well on this inn that I'm going to have to develop another white elephant for a tax write-off.''

Lisa winked at Clinton as he gave her a discreet thumbs-up.

''However,'' Jennifer continued, ''I think it's time for me to leave. You'll be closing in the middle of October anyway, after Thanksgiving weekend, and I think you'll be in good shape for the spring.''

Lisa's happy world closed down. Oh, yes, Clinton had told her the job was seasonal, but she, in her optimism, had managed to forget it. When she didn't forget it completely, she assumed now the inn was doing so well, everybody else would forget it.

The inn couldn't close in October! The car had edged into being twenty percent hers instead of only ten percent; the student loans were steadily dwindling. But that wouldn't continue if she didn't have a job.

She'd have to move back to Halifax, and live with her parents. She'd undoubtedly have to put her name on substitute lists, then start listening for the phone early every morning, and fight for control in the type of classes where students lay in wait like hungry panthers, ready to pounce on new teachers and unwary substitutes.

She wouldn't even blame them if they turned up in class expecting to learn physics or calculus or biology.

Nothing to do, of course, with how she felt about Clinton. Yes, she'd been keeping professional distance lately, but that didn't mean her heart didn't palpitate every time he came within six feet of her.

"Close in October!" Lisa exclaimed to Clinton after Jennifer left. Clinton sat at one end of the big sofa and Lisa loitered on the other. "We can't possibly close in October."

"Look at it this way," he said. "We can't possibly stay open after October. In case you hadn't noticed, Nova Scotia isn't exactly a world-class winter vacation spot. And, let's face it, what traveling salesman is going to stay here in January?"

"But you can't," she said. "You just can't."

"Why can't I, Lisa?"

She couldn't tell him her real reason. Their relationship hadn't progressed quite that far—not by a million miles. Even if it had, he was supposed to say it first. He was supposed to say something like, "Darling, I love you madly. Marry me and be my love and come to Toronto with me." After that he'd tell her all about himself and apologize for not having told her earlier.

Finally she burst out, "What will I do for a job?"

Clinton shrugged. "What everybody else does, I guess? Collect unemployment insurance and come back in the spring. I told you when I hired you it was a seasonal job."

"I know," she said. "But I thought—well, we've done so well, and—"

"Do you seriously expect me to keep this place open without customers just so you'll have a job? Anyway, as soon as you find a teaching position, you're gone. Right?"

"No," she said. "No, I'm not. I love what I'm doing. I can't leave."

Besides that, with the numbers of last year's layoffs, the chances of getting a teaching job this side of the Amazon River were something less than zero.

Aloud she said, "There has to be a way to make this place pay year-round."

He shrugged again. "Go ahead," he said. "Run some ideas by me. But the Snowbirds aren't going to change their minds and hang around here to play 45s instead of going to Florida. Trust me."

Her resentment simmered and boiled over. Clinton didn't take her seriously. He never had. He was just humoring her. Instead of firing her the first night, he'd comforted her because he felt sorry for her, and probably because she still did his typing. After that, he'd been mildly astonished by her success, but she doubted if he felt she made a difference in anything.

She'd show him yet. But first she had to convince him to keep the inn open. She couldn't show him if he were in Toronto and she were in Halifax.

She moved to the chair beside the fire, and turned her face away so he couldn't see how important this was to her.

"Well," she said, "what about conventions? Maybe we could advertise for conventions."

"Sorry," he said. "I think the big hotels in Halifax have that market cornered."

"Well, then, what about staying open just weekends? I can turn my hiking trails into cross-country ski trails and we'll advertise ski packages."

"Our little hiking trails wouldn't satisfy the cross-country ski crowd for long. Also, we'd need rental equipment, and that would mean a big investment for the limited return."

"I know," she said. "Mystery weekends. Aren't those popular?"

"In limited doses," he agreed, "but there's already an inn in the area doing those, and I don't think it makes for good business relations to start undercutting local competitors."

He added with a slight edge to his voice, "Besides, do you know anything about mystery weekends? Have you even been to one? If you had mystery weekends, where would you get the stories?"

"Well, uh," she said, "I guess you just find an old mystery and then make it into a play and then you, uh, give people parts, and . . ."

"Who does this writing?"

"Well, uh, I guess I do."

"And how much do you know about putting on plays?"

"I already told you that I was active in drama in college, that I did a lot of work backstage, and that I was Jessica in *The Merchant of Venice*. I still remember the lines."

"Oh, yes, right. I think you did mention it on that résumé I didn't read, as well as the day you showed me what you looked like at sixteen. Well, I'm sorry to dampen your enthusiasm. Maybe you could carry it off, but I'm afraid that market's saturated. So, unless you think of something really new and smashing—"

She pondered for a moment.

"Oh, oh—idea!" She pointed straight up with one hand and bounced on the chair.

"Yes?"

"I know. We won't have mystery weekends." She drew her legs up and wrapped her arms around her knees and turned to face him. "You're right. Everybody's having them. I know what we'll do. We'll have romance weekends. I haven't heard of anybody doing that. That will attract the young singles crowd and then when they meet each other and get married and have children they'll come back for family weekends and—"

"Whoa! Slow down there," Clinton interrupted, laughing. "I've seen lots of brochures from resorts advertising romance weekends."

"No, no," Lisa said. "Not like those. Those are *romantic* weekends. You know—atmosphere. Moonlit nights and cozy fires and sandy beaches. I mean a real *romance* weekend."

"All right, all right. Exactly what is a romance weekend? As I remember, last time we had a young couple here who wanted a romance weekend, you insisted they pass grapefruits under their chins to perfect strangers and then learn to play 45s."

He reached out an arm, as if to coax her to him, but she turned her face away again.

"Lisa," he said. "Come here." He stood, grasped one of her hands, and pulled her over to where he'd been sitting. He sat down and drew her down beside him.

Yes, she should struggle away, but she couldn't force herself to do that. Anyway, he seemed in the mood to listen to her idea. She didn't want to do anything to interfere with that.

If he didn't listen, they'd be parting soon anyway and the problem would disappear.

Besides, when he touched her, she had absolutely no willpower. She sighed and collapsed against him, tucking her feet up under her.

"Now do you want to explain to me just what a romance weekend is?" he asked.

"Well," she said, "mystery weekends dramatize a mystery story, and gives people parts. The guests then act out the story. They create plays rather than just watching them. Right?"

"Yes, I guess so. Right."

"So, we'll do the same thing, except that instead of starting with a mystery novel or story, we'll start with a romance. We'll dramatize a romance, and then the guests will take parts. That's original, isn't it?"

"Yes. I think that's original. Now, where are you going to get these stories to dramatize?"

"Well," she said, "I read a lot of romance novels, and—"

"Do you now?" he teased. "Somehow I thought that Elizabeth Louise read only Plato, in the original Greek, and, of course, Dostoyevsky and Tolstoy in the original Russian."

Lisa started to bristle.

"Never mind, never mind," he said hastily. "I wouldn't have liked Elizabeth Louise very well anyway. I like Lisa a lot better, romance novels and all. So, go on."

"I'll just take one of the novels I've read and turn it into a play."

"Copyright law. Do you have any idea of how to go about getting permission to turn one of those novels into a play? Or any idea how much it would cost, or how long it would take?"

"Well, no. I don't. So how do you go about it? How much would it cost? How long would it take?"

He shrugged. "Don't ask me. You're the social director. Let's just forget that part of it for the moment. You speak as if turning a book into a play is something you can toss off in fifteen minutes. Have you ever written a play?''

''Well, no. But remember, I've done a lot of things here I'd never done before.''

''Nothing quite that ambitious,'' he commented dryly. ''Then once you get this play written, have you thought out how you're going to set up the romance weekend? How are you going to advertise it? How are you going to decide what people get what parts? What are you going to do about people who just want to play bridge? Have you thought about all these things?''

She hadn't. She hadn't really thought about it at all. The idea had popped into her head, and she'd started talking about it.

She thought fast.

''Maybe we could, well, find a hero and heroine from somewhere to take the main parts. Maybe we could offer them a free weekend at the inn in return for them taking the parts.''

''Any idea of where you'll find these people?''

''Well,'' she said, ''maybe unemployed actors or else students from a drama program at one of the universities. It would be really good experience for a student.

''And,'' she added, ''the other thing is that this is your inn. I'm trying my best to come up with ideas to make it work and all you do is find problems.''

He winced. ''Okay, okay. I'm sorry. Yes, I suppose maybe university students would be interested. How would you contact them?''

''An ad in the paper?'' Her forehead puckered with thought. ''Oh, I know. We could make the same ad do double duty: advertise the romance weekends and offer a free weekend for two people, chosen from applicants, to play the hero and heroine.''

"Okay, Lisa," he said, "I think maybe that part of it does have possibilities. Now, back to the story."

"Are you sure I can't just take a romance I've read?"

"Yes, Lisa. I'm sure. This inn has enough problems without us being thrown into court because you plagiarized a romance novel."

"But that must be what the mystery ones do."

"Who knows? Maybe they've been lucky, and then again, maybe they use mysteries published long enough ago that copyright has run out. Do you think you can find romances that old?"

"No," she said, "no, I don't think so. And if I could, romances that old wouldn't appeal to today's audiences."

She swung her feet off the sofa and tugged her hand free of his. She turned to him, struck a pose with her hand over her heart, and drawled, "Would they, Mr. Daniels?" She lowered her head and batted her eyelashes. "I mean— Clinton."

He laughed. "Right. I don't think the Victorian romance will appeal to today's audiences even if Victorian mysteries do. So what do you suggest?"

She tapped a fingernail against a white and even front tooth while she thought. Finally, she lit up.

"I know!" she said. "I could just write one!"

"You could *what?*"

"Why not?" she said, on the defensive. "I studied creative writing in university, and I am an English major, after all, and—"

She thought he was going to laugh at her again, but instead he said, "Well, maybe you can at that. Anybody who

could create Elizabeth Louise, complete with mink coats
and wolfhounds . . .''

He leaned forward and took both her hands in his, then
looked straight into her eyes.

"All right," he said. "Why don't you just do that? Go
right ahead.

"So—Lisa, write me a romance."

She continued to sit pensively before the fire after Clinton left. Did this mean she had permission? If so, she'd
better put her money where her mouth was. Somehow, between bus tours, and hikes, and card parties, she had to
write and script her romances.

If it didn't work—if she had a money-losing flop—it
would affect not only the coming season but also the long-
term reputation of the inn, to say nothing of her being able
to pay for her car and stay close to Clinton.

It had to work. Whether or not it did was in her hands.

Also, Clinton's comments about the romance novels
stung. If Clinton Daniels thought she was an intellectual
lightweight, she had news for him. Romance novels were
relaxing and they were fun, but she'd show him that her
reading interests didn't stop there. Maybe it was time to
read the Ibsen she had borrowed.

Clinton went back to his apartment, beating himself up
mentally. He'd just made a bad business decision. He
shouldn't have given in to Lisa on the romance weekends.
The whole thing would be a disaster; the inn would lose
the credibility it had built up. The only reason he'd supported it was that it kept Lisa with him.

Policy of noninvolvement! He'd become involved with
Lisa from the night they'd sat and watched the moonlight
glimmer on the river, and since then he'd become as crazy

about her as a sixteen-year-old with his first crush. Regardless of his jokes about collecting unemployment, the thought of going back to Toronto and leaving her in Halifax was unbearable. He couldn't take her to Toronto with him until he was entrenched there rather than galloping all over North America to wherever an inn needed his help. Lisa was the type of woman a man wanted to take care of and come home to every night.

She was creative and unpredictable. She was sweet and kind and he loved her. She loved him too, he knew. The way she responded to his kisses proved that.

Today, for the first time in ages, she'd actually let him touch her again. *Take it slow this time,* he told himself. *Don't scare her away again by coming on too strong.*

"So what do you think?" Lisa said to Clinton a few days later as they sat in her office. She perched behind her desk, and Clinton sprawled in the easy chair she'd requisitioned for herself out of the supply that came for the motel rooms.

"Is it okay to advertise romance weekends for six months—the middle of October through the middle of May? And at the same time ask for applications for the two free spots each time?"

No, it wasn't okay. It wasn't okay at all. His reputation depended on how well his inns performed.

But then, which was more important, money or Lisa?

In fact, he'd begun to wonder if he really wanted to spend the rest of his life as a CEO, making some big company even bigger, working eighteen hours a day, making more and more money that he had no time to spend. Maybe it was his new priorities that were wrong rather than his old ones.

He hedged. "How many different romances are you planning to do?"

"Well," she said, "I thought I'd run each one for four weeks. Maybe next year I can do more."

"If there *is* a next year," said Clinton cynically. He'd somehow assumed Lisa planned to do one script, or, at most, two. She, obviously, was thinking in terms of six.

Lisa, he wanted to say, *are you out of your mind? There will not be a next year. Because of this little caper, you'll be out of a job permanently, and I'll be cruising through a million different inns forever. And I will not be able to marry you and live with you in one place until Jennifer, Silas, and my father all die and I inherit the company. I am decent enough a human being that I sincerely hope that will not happen for another hundred years.*

Chapter Seven

Clinton gazed into Lisa's big brown eyes—so sweet, so enthusiastic, so irresistible. So stubborn.

This would never do. The woman was, after all, his employee, a fact she'd recently insisted that both of them remember.

He stood up, jammed his hands into his pockets, and began to pace. Two steps, hit a wall, turn, two steps, hit another wall.

It made the role of dignified employer very difficult.

He cleared his throat. "Lisa, do you realize you've just committed yourself to the equivalent of writing and scripting a book per month for six months, to say nothing of planning how you're going to present this, and then pulling it off? To say nothing of your regular duties?"

"Yes. I realize that. I can do it."

"You do realize that you're not to neglect your regular duties?"

"Yes, I realize that. Including typing and sewing, I suppose?"

He permitted himself a half-smile. "We can probably negotiate the sewing."

Lisa put her hands on her hips. "Very generous," she said. "I notice you didn't offer to negotiate the typing."

"No," he said. "I'm not negotiating the bookkeeping or the mail either. Now, tell me—have you ever in your life written a book?"

At least she had the grace to look at her fingernails and blush. "Well, no," she said.

"And what is the longest piece of writing you have done?"

"Other than the term paper on the Spanish Inquisition? In my creative writing course, our final assignment was a twenty-page short story." She continued to examine her nails. "For your information, I got an A on it and the professor read it out loud in class."

"Very impressive."

"There's no need to be sarcastic."

"Yeah, right. Now. How long are these romances you've read a lot of?"

"About two hundred pages," she admitted. "But it would be more like a screenplay, and they're not as long. And this would be my main job now. Once these start we won't have any regular work during the week."

"No, that's true," he commented dryly, "except for fall foliage bus tours, and continuing to teach the seniors how to play cards, and clearing more hiking trails, and—"

"—and typing and bookkeeping and mail," she said. "And are you sure about the sewing? Maybe you'd like drapes for the forty-eight or so rooms in the imaginary second story."

She jumped to her feet, face flaming. "Clinton Daniels, all you do is criticize. I haven't heard you come up with any ideas. What do you think we should do for the winter?"

"I told you that long ago. Close up and collect unemployment."

Lisa had steam coming out her ears, figuratively speaking. "What a cop-out," she stormed. "Don't you have any imagination? Any—any—*anything*?"

"All right, Lisa," Clinton said. "Why don't you sit down, Ms. Flamethrower?" He stopped pacing and sat on the corner of her desk. "Just remember. You're an employee here. At any moment you might get a teaching job and take off, leaving me with the last five books to write and script for all these romantic weekends we advertised."

"*Romance* weekends!"

"Whatever. Or, if it doesn't go well, you can just quit. You might have had the idea, but I'm the one who has to live with the results. I'm the one who will end up with egg all over my face if it doesn't work out. Have you thought of that?"

"No." She sat down again, facing him over the desktop. "No, I hadn't. All right. If you'll go ahead on this, I promise I won't run off, not even if the queen offers me a job tutoring some of her grandchildren. I will see the romance weekends through until the last scheduled one the middle of May unless I'm dead. Are you satisfied?"

"How do I know that's true?"

"I swear it, on my honor!"

He couldn't help it. He chuckled. "On the honor of Elizabeth Louise, she of the imaginary height, the imaginary coloring, the imaginary mink coats, and the imaginary dogs?"

"No. On the honor of Lisa. Now are you satisfied?"

"Not really. But I haven't thought of anything better."

The bottom line was that he couldn't deny Lisa anything she wanted.

"Give it your best shot, kid." He held out his hands, and they slapped palms.

"Thank you, Clinton," she said fervently, "thank you so much. I won't let you down."

"Come in," Lisa said in response to the knock on her office door. Clinton walked in.

He picked up the wooden chair that sat in front of the card table, moved it to her desk, placed it backwards, and then sat straddling it, arms resting on the back.

Lisa stared at her laptop.

"So how's the great author doing?"

"My heroine's going to be blond," she said.

"Uh-huh. Surprise. And statuesque, right? And named Elizabeth Louise? Right?"

"Oh." She pushed aside the mouse. How maddening he was.

"Yes," she said. "That's right. Right on all counts."

"Well, then, you're going to need a villainess, aren't you? And if the heroine is blond and statuesque, what's the villainess going to look like?" He scrutinized her. "Are you going to have a fresh-faced, perky, dimpled villainess, with merry brown eyes? Now, that will never do."

"Well," she said, "I am going to have a blond statuesque heroine, and a dark handsome hero."

"And what's your story going to be about?"

She thought fast. The truth was she'd stared at the blank screen for two days now, and she still had no idea what the story would be about.

"It's going to be about love," she said.

"That sort of goes without saying, doesn't it? But what's it going to be about besides love?"

A wild idea hit her. "It's going to take place in this area—you know—local color. And it's going to be about, about—Gypsies."

Well, she certainly had his attention.

"Gypsies! Gypsies? In this area? With a blond, statuesque heroine? Where are you getting this blond statuesque heroine from? Gypsies, you know, are dark."

She'd never created so fast in her life. The problem was, she'd be stuck with what she created. Clinton would never let her live it down if she changed. Anyway, she hadn't come up with any ideas to change to.

"The heroine isn't really a Gypsy," she improvised. "The heroine was stolen by Gypsies when she was a small child and she grew up to be a startling beauty who is wooed by the wicked Gypsy king. And the Gypsy king's daughter, with dark and flashing eyes, intends to marry the hero, the handsome young Gypsy the heroine loves."

Her imagination took over and she rushed on enthusiastically. "But then, you see," she finished, "the hero and the heroine do find each other, and, guess what—she's really the daughter of the mayor of Mahone Bay. Guess who the hero is?"

"I don't know. The manager of The Lunenburg Whaler?"

"No!" She shot him a triumphant look, and slapped her palm on the desk. "He's really the son of a British nobleman, and the Gypsies kidnapped him in England before they came to Mahone Bay."

She finished, "They got married and lived happily ever after."

"Lisa," Clinton said, his voice kind, "I don't want to hurt your feelings, but that's the silliest story I ever heard."

"All right, then," she said between her teeth, "if that's the silliest story you've ever heard, why don't you try this one on for size?

"Some guy gets shipwrecked on an island with his infant daughter. He takes up magic out of boredom. He releases a fairy that was trapped in a tree trunk and the fairy becomes his general handyman and message boy, even though there aren't a lot of messages on the island.

"Eventually the daughter grows up, and needs a husband, so daddy conjures up a storm to wreck a handsome prince for her. However, he makes the prince carry wood first just to be sure he's good enough for the daughter. Then when the prince passes the wood-carrying test, the prince and the daughter get married and everybody lives happily ever after, including the fairy and the guys who drowned in the shipwreck. Do you like that one better?"

He chuckled. "I guess maybe they're about tied, at that."

"Well, for your information, I can't use the second one. It's already been done, and I'd hate to run afoul of copyright laws. It was written by some guy named William Shakespeare, but I don't suppose that name rings a bell with you, so I—I—" She got to her feet and began to sail proudly out.

The main problem with sailing out was that the office was so small she had to edge her way past Clinton. He caught her wrist gently and stopped her. Swinging smoothly out of his chair, and still holding Lisa by the wrist, he moved into the easy chair under the window and pulled her down onto his lap.

"Hey—lady. I'm qualified to teach university-level English, remember. Somewhere, buried in the depths of my subconscious, the name William Shakespeare just does ring a bell.

"Now what are you planning to name this thirty-day wonder?"

"Hmm," she said. "What about *The Gypsies of Mahone Bay*? That has a catchy sound."

"Well," Clinton admitted, "certainly catchier than *The Gypsies of Chester*, or *The Gypsies of New Ross*. Okay, put out your advertising for your romance weekends, with *The Gypsies of Mahone Bay* to run the first four weekends, third weekend in October through the second weekend in November."

He brushed his fingers across her mouth, and drew her close. When he ran his lips over her hair, she didn't resist, but instead relaxed against him, and rested her head against his shoulder. He stroked her hair.

"I'm sorry I made fun of you. You've turned everything else in this outfit to gold. You'll probably pull this one off, too. Now what did you say the name of the heroine is?"

She snuggled against him. He was strong and warm and smelled of aftershave.

"Her real name," she said, "is Elizabeth Louise Romanov. I haven't thought yet of the Gypsies' name for her."

He nuzzled her neck. "Look, why don't the Gypsies just call her Lisa? And why don't you just give her dark hair and dimples and merry brown eyes?"

She sighed and moved one of her arms around his neck.

"That's better," he whispered, as he cupped her chin in one hand and tipped her face up to his. "Now, let's get you in the mood for writing romance."

* * *

Lisa went to bed with Henrik Ibsen. She hoped he'd put her to sleep, but he didn't. As she scanned the pages of *A Doll's House,* she felt as if Ibsen were talking to her. He'd written the play over a hundred years ago, but he was talking now to Lisa.

Nora Helmer's husband treated her like a doll, constantly told her not to trouble her empty head about things that were the proper sphere of males.

Yet when her husband was ill, Nora went to a money-lender for the money to save his life, and did secretarial work, in secret, to meet the payments. Because she was a woman, she could get the loan only by forging her father's name. When the moneylender discovered this, and used the information to blackmail her husband, the husband she'd saved became enraged. When the threat was withdrawn, she was once more the pet, the doll, the singing bird, the empty-headed woman.

No wonder the woman left him.

Her own stakes were not as high as Nora's, Lisa admitted, but in many ways *she* was Nora, coddled by her father and now patronized by Clinton, expected to look pretty and have an empty head. When she did do something worthwhile, did Clinton give her credit?

Let's face it, Lisa. People staying at a motel don't want to be entertained. I hired you for yours skills in typing and sewing. Be a good little girl, Lisa, and run along and live on unemployment insurance over winter. Then maybe you can type and sew for me again in the spring.

Clinton might be tempted to love her, but he didn't really respect her. Oh, yes, he respected her in the sense of not taking advantage of her, but he didn't respect *her*, her brain, her abilities, her identity as a unique human being.

He didn't even respect her enough to be honest about his position with S and J.

The Gypsies of Mahone Bay became reality. September and early October disappeared faster than autumn leaves in a windstorm, but somehow Lisa managed the script on time— between hikes and bus tours and card games. The fall program had become unexpectedly popular.

The advertising for the hero and heroine didn't have the success Lisa had anticipated. She had just one application, complete with picture, for the part of the heroine. It came from Halifax. One Helene Heatherstone, unemployed, had once upon a time had a bit part in a Neptune Theatre production.

Lisa sighed. She had no choice but to give Helene Heatherstone the job. She looked at the picture. It was a glamor shot, probably taken years ago, but even at that Ms. Heatherstone looked as if she'd never see forty again. The character of Elizabeth Louise was nineteen. However, Lisa comforted herself, makeup—especially theatrical makeup— could do wonders.

She squelched the thought that the main thing theatrical makeup would do at such close quarters would be to look frightfully like theatrical makeup.

There were positives, she assured herself. Helene Heatherstone was tall and thin, and, at least at the time the picture was taken, blond. She seemed very eager to come.

There'd been no applications for the hero. In desperation, Lisa phoned a drama professor she knew and asked for names, and then phoned the names on the list. Finally, one third-year drama student accepted reluctantly, and even sent a photograph and a brief résumé. He was tall, dark, and more or less handsome. True, he looked far more like Helene's son than her lover.

Lisa mentally outlined the procedure. There would be performances on Friday and Saturday evenings and on Sunday afternoon. The parts would be switched around, even the lead parts if there were guests who were willing and able. All she needed were enough registered guests to pull it off.

She went home for two days in the middle of the week and spent most of her time in the public library, poring over pictures of Gypsy costumes, reading about Gypsy history for background, and making lists of Gypsy names. Flamenco music, she noted, was attributed to Gypsies.

She bought clothes and cheap costume jewelry in secondhand stores; she bought materials and sewing supplies and several records of violin and flamenco music. She brought all these back to the inn.

In a pique of rebellion, an affirmation of her own identity, defying the mild weather and the lack of access to rinks, she also brought her ice skates.

Now, she'd spend all her free moments taping Gypsy music and sewing baggy pants and voluminous skirts.

Her relationship with Clinton was a combination of easy friendship and casual contact.

That, she assured herself, was just the way she wanted it.

If I could just propose, and put us both out of our misery, Clinton thought. He'd no doubt about her answer. The state of things now surely had become as frustrating to her as it was to him. He wanted Lisa totally and forever, complete with wedding band and babies.

Somehow, since Samantha's defection, he'd thought of

marriage as something that would happen sometime. Maybe when he was thirty-five; maybe when he was forty. Certainly not when he was twenty-nine.

Marriage came with a split-level and spacious grounds. It came with two people who were home every night, not with a husband rocketing around the world from one failing inn to the next.

When he'd lied about his financial state, he'd wanted to be sure that she, too, didn't have her eye on the main chance. Later? Lies once told became difficult to undo later.

She'd told him, theoretically of course, that she thought a couple should work together to build a future. But, regardless of how she perceived herself, she was sweet and feminine and traditional—the type of woman every man wanted to take care of.

He couldn't ask her to make a commitment. After all, this time next year, he could be in Peru. But he couldn't let her go. They were still together, working together, playing together—when his willpower totally packed it in, cuddling and kissing together. For now, he supposed, he'd continue to drift and hope she didn't give up on him by the time he was ready for marriage.

Or maybe, he should forget all about inns and getting ahead. That thought was occurring on a regular basis. Maybe he could get a job teaching high school English in some place too remote to have heard of cutbacks. Life in Yellowknife, or Inuvik, or Resolute Bay, might not be so bad if he could spend the long arctic nights with Lisa.

He shook his head as if to sort out an addled brain. Maybe he should just forget about Lisa.

Helene Heatherstone appeared in time for Friday lunch. Clinton and Lisa stood at the lobby window watching the swirl of autumn leaves on a golden day, the Friday of the third weekend in October.

"Who is that?" Clinton said, as a car, half the size and twice the age of the *Titanic*, swept up the driveway.

"I don't know," Lisa said, "but whoever it is appears to be driving an 1870 Cadillac."

"Lisa, there's no such thing as an 1870 Cadillac."

"I know. But that still looks like what she's driving." The car was close enough now for them to determine that the driver and lone occupant was a woman.

"Our leading lady," they said in unison, and turned and looked at each other.

The woman parked the car and climbed out, dripping rabbit skins disguised as mink. Perched jauntily over one eye, she wore a little fur hat of the style popular during the Second World War. It was also rabbit disguised as mink.

"Or maybe it really is mink," Clinton said. "I think mink was cheaper sixty years ago."

She stopped on the front steps to light a fresh cigarette and place it in a long cigarette holder of plastic disguised as ivory.

Lisa groaned. "Elizabeth Louise as a bag lady," she said.

Clinton, complete with dark suit and dazzling white shirt, opened the front door and beckoned the leading lady in. "Welcome to The Lunenburg Whaler and 'The Romance Weekend of Your Dreams.' " He bowed low and kissed Helene's hand. "I am Clinton Daniels, manager, and you, I presume, are the enchanting actress, Helene Heatherstone."

Helene fairly purred. "So *dee*-lighted to meet you-all, dahling. And this little lady behind you is . . ."

Clinton's dimple began to twitch.

Oh, no you don't. Before Clinton could open his mouth, Lisa moved smoothly in front of him and put out her hand. "I'm Lisa Bannerman," she said, "social and recreation director for the inn. Welcome to The Lunenburg Whaler, Ms. Heatherstone. I'm so glad you were able to make it."

"Oh, dahling, how sweet," Helene said to Lisa as she smiled at Clinton. "Ah do hope you-all are successful. Ah'm so happy to be heah at your little play. Ah was between jobs, you-all know, and ah thought it might be amusing to spend a weekend in rural Nova Scotia, before Ah'm called back to New York."

"Let me show you to your room, Ms. Heatherstone," said Clinton, "so you can settle in before lunch." He offered her his arm and the two of them swept out, Helene scattering *dahlings* and ashes behind her as she went.

Thank goodness, Lisa thought, as a steady stream of guests checked in. There were enough.

She felt uncomfortable as she remembered Clinton's words, *"That's the silliest story I've ever heard,"* and even more uncomfortable when she thought of the leading lady, a forty-something painted has-been. No, not even a has-been. She never was.

To add to Lisa's problems, the leading man had not appeared. Lisa stood in the lobby all afternoon, greeting guests as they arrived, but no one among them was the leading man. All the guests expected had arrived.

Lisa stayed in the lobby, the hero's script in her hand, nose pressed against the glass of the door, wondering however she could run this show without a leading man. There had to be someone who had some idea of theater to get the thing rolling. Otherwise it would fall flat on its face.

She was about to give up and go to dinner when a motorcycle turned into the driveway and roared up it at full speed, at the last moment swinging in beside the old Cadillac in a spray of gravel.

I hope he didn't damage Ms. Heatherstone's antique paint, Lisa thought spitefully. *On the car, that is.*

The young man strolled up to the door, helmet in hand. The helmet was the only concession to his vehicle. He wore blue jeans and tennis shoes. Lisa winced. She hadn't even thought about shoes when she bought and made costumes.

She swung open the door and smiled.

"Welcome to The Lunenburg Whaler and 'The Romance Weekend of Your Dreams.' "

"Hi." He stuck out his free hand and clutched hers. "I'm Adam Adken. You asked me to come and play the hero for your romantic weekend, remember? I'm really looking forward to this. I think it's going to be a lot of fun. And then I think any experience I'm able to get is valuable. I hope I'm in time. My last class ran until four o'clock so I had to hustle right down. Gee, I really am looking forward to this."

"Yes," she said, as she removed her hand from his, wiggling it to restore circulation. "I'm very pleased to meet you. Won't you come in, and I'll show you to your room. Oh, and here's your script." She handed it to him, and hustled him down the hall.

At least he'd shown up. It seemed small compensation. He was very young, he was tall and dark but more than a little plump, and he looked more like Helene's grandson than her son, never mind her lover. True, theatrical makeup could do miracles, but not likely miracles of this magnitude.

Lisa had transformed the dining room into her version of a Gypsy camp, complete with pictures of caravans and Gypsy dancers, and a violin propped on top of the dessert cart. Before and during dinner she played taped Gypsy violin music. She'd changed into Gypsy costume and had bulldozed Clinton and Helene into doing the same.

The other costumes were draped over unused chairs. There were baggy pants (waists elasticized to fit all sizes), bright shirts, vests, and sashes for the men, and colorful skirts and blouses for the women and an abundance of multipurpose scarves in all the shades of the rainbow.

At the beginning of dinner, Lisa briefly described the play and the characters, then explained how parts would be allotted. When the meal was over, she handed out scripts and costumes, and gave instructions for anyone wanting a touch of makeup to turn up at 7:30. Then she cornered the two stars with her makeup kit.

"But, dahling," protested Helene, "Ah'm gorgeous just as Ah am."

"Oh, yes, Ms. Heatherstone, but we have to have some way of telling the professionals from the amateurs, don't we? We don't want these other people to think you're just a highly talented guest, do we now?"

"Well, dahling, putting it that way—"

Lisa gritted her teeth and hoped that a half-inch of greasepaint would hide the wrinkles of the leading lady, and that a few artificial lines and a moustache might keep the leading man from looking like a very tall but plumpish ten-year-old.

Everybody had appeared by eight, in costume. The extras sat on the floor in the rosy glow of the make-believe campfire.

The violin music started and the Gypsy king sauntered

on, with the violin from the dessert table tucked under his chin.

He was an insurance salesman, outgoing and enthusiastic. He'd come at 7:30 for makeup and insisted on a moustache and a black patch over one eye. He wore a single gold earring, borrowed from his wife. Whether he looked more like a Gypsy king or the pirate from an operetta was questionable, but he added dash and flair.

He waved his bow for emphasis, holding it and the script in the same hand. He squinted at his script. ''I am Gunari, zee Gypsy king,'' he announced. ''I will have zee beautiful blond maiden we call Simza for my feeth wife.''

He wiggled his upper lip in a vain attempt to twirl his moustache, then sprung into the air and clicked his heels twice before exiting.

The two lovers scampered on, Helene drowning in makeup. Lisa had drawn her hair into two ponytails in a failed attempt to make her look younger.

Lisa stood by the door with Clinton and scraped at her nail polish.

''I am Elizabeth Louise Romanov,'' began Helene dramatically. ''My father is the mayor of Mahone Bay, and I, alas, woe is me, I, who am the most beautiful woman Mahone Bay has ever seen, I was kidnapped by Gypsies as a mere child. A very beautiful mere child, mind you,'' she libbed.

''Now that I have grown into a very beautiful young woman, the beautiful woman the Gypsies call Simza, I am being forced to marry the ugly, dirty Gypsy king,'' she said, rolling her eyes to the ceiling, ''old enough to be my father.''

''Your son, you mean,'' muttered Clinton, *sotto voce*, and Lisa said ''Sssh'' under her voice.

"His last six wives," Helene went on.

"Four, you idiot," muttered Lisa.

"Sssh," said Clinton, "and anyway, does it matter?"

"His last eight wives," said Helene, "have vanished in mysterious circumstances."

"And I, my sweetest love," began Adam in a treble squeak which slid into bass once he got started, "I, whom the Gypsies call Shandor, am being pursued by his daughter, the dark and evil Luludja."

Lisa groaned. "It's even worse than I thought," she whispered to Clinton. "His voice is still changing!"

"That's all right," Clinton whispered back, "his child bride will never notice."

"Sssh," whispered Lisa.

"Oh, yes," bellowed the leading lady, "his ugly daughter, Luludja."

"Never fear, my chaste and lovely darling, my darling whom the Gypsies call fair Simza, I will carry you far from here before either of them can get their slimy paws on us."

"Oh, how awful," Lisa moaned aloud as she shut her eyes, and hid her face on Clinton's shoulder. He put a comforting arm around her.

How embarrassing. How could she ever have written that drivel? She could never face anybody again.

What would happen to the rest of the romance weekends, already heavily advertised? What would happen to the inn? What would happen to her? What would happen to Clinton's reputation? There were only two bright spots. She'd had second thoughts about inviting her parents, and the local newspaper reporter whom she had invited couldn't make it.

Clinton stood with Lisa's head on his shoulder, and his

arm around her. He ran his hand up and down her back, comforting her.

She heard laughter, and buried her head a little deeper. Of course they were laughing. They were going to laugh her right out of here.

"Come on, Lisa," Clinton said. "Just look at them." He forced his free hand against her chin, and made her look at the crowd.

She couldn't believe it. They were having fun. Yes, they were laughing, but they were laughing because they were having such a good time.

The hero and heroine exaggerated their words, and rolled their eyes, and crossed their arms and executed little introductory flamenco steps whenever they approached each other. Helene stomped her heels on the floor, and Adam responded as best he could in tennis shoes. Their enthusiasm and that of the Gypsy king lit sparks in the others.

The Gypsy king made his next entrance with a bread knife from the kitchen held in his teeth. His daughter flamencoed her way around all the tables, removing the flowers from the vases and tucking them in her hair, until she looked more like King Lear in his mad scene than she did like a Gypsy princess.

The Gypsy king, unwilling to be upstaged, put down the script and the violin and the bread knife, crossed his arms, sat on his heels, and did a wild Cossack dance.

Lisa caught a quick little breath and looked up at Clinton. He beamed down at her, absolutely beamed. He hugged her and quoted, "You've done it! By George, and by Elizabeth Louise, you've done it!"

Chapter Eight

After the performance, the guests crowded around Lisa, congratulating her, looking forward to the next night and to Sunday afternoon, badgering her about the next five plays. She smiled and beamed and chatted and told them she didn't want to spoil the surprise, not wanting to admit she hadn't even started to think about the Christmas play, never mind the four after that.

Afterward she sat with Clinton on the front steps, breathing the balmy night air, and looking at the full moon. Her resolve to keep their relationship professional was forgotten in the glow of her success.

She sat on the step below him, her interlaced hands resting on one of his knees and her cheek lying against her hands. He caressed her hair, running his finger along the edge of the feathery bangs.

She raised her head and sighed. ''Have you ever seen a

130

moon like that?'' she asked. ''In all your life, have you ever seen a moon like that?''

''Hmm.'' He quoted:

'' 'The moon shines bright: in such a night as this,
When the sweet wind did gently kiss the trees
And they did make no noise, in such a night
Troilus methinks mounted the Troyan walls
And sigh'd his soul toward the Grecian tents,
Where Cressid lay that night.' ''

''Well,'' she said. ''Mr. ex-English prof, you've made your point. You have heard of Shakespeare, but you're not the only one. I can quote too, you know. Remember, I had the part of Jessica in college, and I still remember the lines.''

''You look like a Jessica, you know, small and dark and intense. Anyway, go on. Quote me your quote.''

She hitched herself up to the next step, leaned her head against Clinton's chest, and gazed at the moon.

'' 'In such a night
Did Thisbe fearfully o'er trip the dew,
And saw the lion's shadow ere himself
And ran dismay'd away.' ''

''Yes,'' he said, ''you did it,'' and continued:

''In such a night
Stood Lisa with a greasepaint in her hand
Upon the dining room table and waft her love
To come again to Chester.''

"I can call you and raise you," she said.

"In such a night
Elizabeth Louise gather'd the enchanted herbs
That did renew old Helene."

Clinton replied:

"In such a night
Did Lisa steal from The Lunenburg Whaler
And with an unthrift love did run from there
As far as Chester."

Lisa picked up the response:

"In such a night
Did young Clinton swear he loved her well,
Stealing her soul with many vows of faith
And ne'er a true one."

"Aha," he cried, "thou slanderest. Who art thou to say they were not true?"

"Oops," she said. "I guess I got caught up in the game. I didn't mean to say that. I wasn't thinking of the words."

He ran his hand up and down the curve of her throat, where it emerged from the neck of her Gypsy blouse.

"I was," he said, his voice soft and gentle. "You are so lovely, Lisa."

They sat in silence for a moment. She squeezed his hand.

"Thanks," she said. "I guess we should go in," she added. "But I don't want to. This is a magic night."

"What do you want to do?"

"You know what I'd really like to do?"

"What, my Gypsy princess?"

"I'd like to go somewhere and park where the moon shines on the water. And talk, I guess. Anything to keep this beautiful feeling front and center for another hour."

"Consider it done."

She got to her feet. "I'll just run in and change."

"No." He caught her hand, and looked at her standing before him in the low-necked blouse, the voluminous purple skirt, the wide, tightly laced black belt that made her waist look tiny.

"No," he said. "Just stay as you are." He looked down at his own orange and hunter-green Gypsy outfit. "You're beautiful. Just wait a moment while I change."

Clinton drove to Chester and parked the car where the moon reflected on the water.

They sat without speaking in the front seat of the big station wagon. Clinton's arm grazed Lisa's shoulders.

Go somewhere and talk, she'd said. At the time, she'd probably even thought she'd meant it. She didn't want to spend the next hour talking any more than he did.

He turned toward her, and swiveled her so that she faced him. She looked up at him, at the hazel eyes now gazing into her own. With slow and loving fingers, he traced the contours of her face, down her cheek, along her jaw.

Her face shone luminous in the moonlight. Her eyes were black pools, so big and intense he could drown in them. She was so beautiful and so good. He regretted every teasing remark, every put-down he had ever made. How could a man do anything with Lisa but worship at her feet?

He stroked the side of her neck and the curve of her throat. Her white neck gleamed like ivory in the moonlight, and his touch was almost reverent.

"Lisa," he whispered, "you are so lovely, so beautiful, I—" he broke off.

Lisa combed her fingers through his hair. His kisses fell soft as Christmas snow. It seemed they went on forever, as her arms tightened about his neck.

"Lisa, Lisa," he murmured. "Oh, Lisa, I—"

He slowly released her, started the car, and returned to the inn. Then Clinton watched Lisa as she moved down the hall and turned into her room.

Lisa unlaced her Gypsy vest. Clinton had been about to say, *I love you.* They were the words she'd been waiting to hear ever since the night of the restaurant opening. Oh, yes, he teased her without mercy, and sometimes he made her so mad she could explode, but that's just the way he was, and she loved him.

Why didn't he say it? He'd thrown out enough hints. If he'd just come right out and say it, it would solve everything. She went crazy every time he touched her, every time he kissed her, and it was getting worse.

She knew what she wanted. She wanted to marry him and live with him forever, but not until he considered her important enough to tell her the things that she'd learned from Jennifer.

On the other side of the wall, Clinton tossed and turned. Sleep evaded him.

He loved Lisa. Yes, he loved her beauty, but he also loved her spirit, her gumption, the way she spit fire back at him when he teased her. He loved her imagination, her wonderful wonderful imagination—the imagination that had invented Elizabeth Louise, the imagination that kept guests coming back to the inn, the imagination that had created *The Gypsies of Mahone Bay*.

His love for her transcended physical desire. He wanted her to be the mother of his children; he'd watched her with the children who came to the inn—on the hiking trails, getting ready for the play in the evening. She loved children, and he wanted her to have his.

But because he loved her, he wanted to give her the best. He would not expect Lisa to spend the next several years traipsing around after him to failing inns. Neither could he bear leaving her at home and being away from her for months on end.

He mused on. Maybe Jennifer would forget about his troubleshooter position and would find a permanent job for him even if it weren't the executive position he'd thought he wanted and deserved. Maybe she'd make him manager of the Dartmouth Inn if he threatened and begged.

Tonight, he'd come close to telling Lisa he loved her, but he'd caught himself in time. That wasn't the way, in the front seat of a car, with the words prompted by hormones. He'd take her to a nice restaurant for dinner— maybe in the city—with candlelight, and fresh flowers, and there, apart from the clinches and the kisses, there in a romantic atmosphere, he'd tell her he loved her, but also tell her he wasn't sure how long it would be before they could be together.

But first, it was sensible to wait until he had a better idea of what he was facing. Jennifer had been cool when he informed her of the romance weekends, but agreed to reserve judgment until she could come down and see for herself.

In the meantime, the only safe approach with Lisa was warm friendship. He had, tonight, in the glow of success after the play, come much too close to blurting out a hurried proposal.

"Ms. Bannerman," said Adam, cornering Lisa in the lobby at the end of lunch.

"Yes."

"Look, Ms. Bannerman," he said, "I hope this doesn't inconvenience you. It was a lot of fun and all that, but the truth is I think I'm cutting out."

"Huh," she said, "I notice you waited until you'd had lunch."

"Now, look, Ms. Bannerman, there's no reason to be huffy."

She laid her hand on his arm. "I'm sorry," she said. "I didn't mean that. It just sort of slipped out. Now, look, Adam, we really need you. You've been absolutely super. It just won't be the same."

"Sorry," he said. "I've got a big date tonight."

"I imagine you didn't just arrange that now. You must have known before. Why did you agree to come?"

He shrugged. "Well, you know, it sounded like a blast. And it was, too. It really was a blast, but I've done it now. And then there were the free meals, and it didn't cost me much to come, what with the bike."

"But you agreed," she said. "You just don't walk out on an agreement. Not unless there's an emergency."

"You don't have anything in writing, do you? Anyway, as I remember, you're the one who begged me to come. I gave you last night, didn't I? Where would your weekend have been without me? You can't complain. Anyway, you promised me a beautiful blond to be my leading lady. That one's old enough to be my mother."

"Grandmother, Adam," Lisa said without thinking.

"Yeah, well, that's true. I didn't want to say it. And every other female here is either somebody's wife or somebody's child. Now, then," he said, looking at her speculatively, "if *you'd* agree to go out with me after the show, and be really nice to me, maybe I could arrange to stay the rest of this weekend if that were the case."

Why, you— she thought.

"Why, you—" she said, "you little jerk. Who do you think you are? Now get out of here—right now, and take your wretched bike," she roared as she pointed to the door, "and your wretched tennis shoes with you. And don't you dare make fun of Helene. She's twice the man that you are."

She turned her back on him and stalked down the hall, thinking only as she heard the roar of the motorcycle a few minutes later, *And good riddance!*

The whole world was the same. Everybody out for himself. The carpenters going on strike; the kitchen staff quitting on the day of the grand opening; then this oversized little twerp, still wet behind the ears.

Reality hit. What would she do? She'd scheduled another show for that evening. True, everybody had had great fun, but the two semiprofessionals had started the ball rolling and kept things on track. The insurance salesman might have been a possibility, but he stayed only one night. He'd left a few hours earlier.

The only thing to do was approach Clinton.

"Oh, no," he said, when she'd hunted him down in the dining room and explained. "Huh-uh, sweetie. No way. I'll go through fire, flood, and war for you. I'll tiptoe through crocodile-infested swamps at your bidding. I'll cuddle you and kiss you and love you, but I will not—I repeat, will not—take the leading part in your little play."

"Clinton," she begged, so desperate she overlooked the word "little," "you have to. You just have to. What will I do?"

"What about the insurance salesman? He was just as good as the pros."

"He left this morning."

"Oh. Any reason? You didn't try to teach him the grape-fruit game?"

"No. He'd planned it that way from the beginning. His reservation was just for Friday night."

"Why me, Lisa? I'm no better than the rest of the crowd. I'm no pro."

"You're almost," she said. "You're an English prof. Don't tell me you went all the way through two arts degrees without any courses in drama or being involved in any plays. Did you?"

"Well—" He hedged. "A bit, maybe. But that was ages ago."

"Besides, it's your inn. As you pointed out to me when all this started, if it fails, I go on to another job and you're stuck with the failure. Don't you have any sense of obligation?"

"Tell you what," he said, after a lengthy pause, "if you'll promise to be really nice to me afterward—"

He broke off as Lisa threw her empty coffee cup at him and stormed out of the dining room, through the lobby, and down the hall. She heard the cup shatter against the fireplace.

He ran after her and caught her as she reached her office door. He grabbed her by the wrist and swung her around.

"Now, then," he demanded, "do you want to tell me what all that was about?"

"Let me go!" she said. "Just let me go. You jerk!"

"Hey, now, just a minute. A little bit of teasing shouldn't bring that reaction. Maybe I used bad judgment teasing you at a time like this, but it still shouldn't be that bad.

"Here," he said, taking away the tissue she was using to dab ineffectually at her eyes, and proceeding to do a much better job. "Now come on."

He led her into her office. "Now, tell me what's really wrong."

"That's what *he* said," she snarled.

"Who said?"

"Adam said. He told me that if I was really nice to him—and I don't think he left me in a lot of doubt about what he meant—" She paced the small room, rhythmically thumping a clenched fist into the open palm of the other hand.

"Oh, for Pete's sake," Clinton said, "it can't be that bad."

"Well, it was." She continued the pacing and thumping. "He told me if I was really nice he'd stay and otherwise he wouldn't, and now you're saying the same thing."

"Come on, Lisa," he said, "there's a big difference. He meant it, didn't he?"

She nodded.

"Now, do you think I meant it?"

She shook her head and sunk into the chair behind her desk.

"No," she said, "I guess not."

"Okay, I'll do it."

"Thank you," she said. "Thank you, thank you, thank you!"

By time Lisa had combed her hair and repaired her makeup, she felt much better. She'd overreacted with Clinton because she was worried and stressed out.

He'd just made a joke. He was a dreadful tease. She'd known that since the day he interviewed her.

But, in spite of his teasing manner, he was a nice person. He'd supported her in this romance weekend idea. If it hadn't been for keeping her employed, he'd have closed for the winter, and gone off to work in one of Jennifer's other, more successful, inns. Besides, every time he looked at her, caressed her, her pulse rate revved up into overdrive.

Enough about Clinton and pulse rates. Put it out of mind. Especially as he still hadn't considered her important enough to tell her who he really was.

Right now, she had another show to think about.

She had to get the dining room ready, repair and iron the costumes, and sort out the scripts. She should have checked the costumes and scripts last night, but she'd been busy kissing Clinton.

Then she should have done them early in the morning, but she'd overslept because she'd been up late kissing Clinton.

After all, she'd been the one who'd suggested going somewhere, so she could hardly insist on going home after half an hour. Anyway, the night was so balmy for this time of year, and the moonlight on the water was so romantic, and Clinton's lips were so gentle. . . .

Lisa made her introductory talk, and then stood in costume in the doorway.

The Gypsy king gave his speech; the lovers came onstage.

Helene bowed low and prostrated herself at Clinton's feet.

"I am being forced to marry the ugly," and she kissed her lover's feet, "dirty," and she kissed the hem of his baggy pants, "Gypsy king," and she kissed his knees, "old enough to be my father," and she clasped him around the waist and, panting, hauled herself to her feet. "His last eight wives," and she turned to the audience saying, "Count with me. *One*," and the extras around the artificial campfire roared *"One"* as she kissed her Gypsy lover once on the lips, *"Two,"* and the extras roared *"Two"* and whistled as she kissed him twice on the lips.

As he spoke the next line, "And I, my sweetest love, am being pursued by his daughter," he knelt on one knee and bent Helene backward over the other one, leaning over her and kissing her passionately. On Helene's next line, the positions were reversed.

Oh. Oh. Clinton and Helene between them had rewritten her play. *Her* play. Without even saying to her, "Here's a new idea we've come up with. What do you think?" Sure, the kisses were the faked stage version, but that wasn't the way they looked. In her play, the kissing had been the chaste version of Victorian romances. Touch the lips. Hold for two seconds. Release. *That* was the kissing in the play she had written, a play for an inn focusing on family weekends, family values.

These changes weren't in the same league as the Gypsy king's daughter putting flowers in her hair, or the insurance salesman dancing with a bread knife in his teeth. These revisions changed the whole tone and focus of *her* play.

Those changes were just the beginning.

She was unreasonably angry. It was just like Ibsen said. Nothing Nora did had any importance; Torvald could just come along and dismiss all her efforts as trivial. It was exactly the same here. Who did Clinton think he was to change what she had written without so much as a by-your-leave?

The whistling and applause went on and on, until Lisa thought her head would split. There was no consolation in the thought that everyone was having a wonderful time and that the performance was going even better than last night's. There was no consolation in the knowledge that Clinton's version of her play was superior to her own.

After it was over, Lisa lingered in the dining room, not wanting to go to her lonely room, not wanting to do anything else. Forlornly, she gathered up costumes and arranged the makeup in neat rows in the makeup kit.

"Hi," Clinton said. He'd already changed from his Gypsy costume into jeans and a sweatshirt.

She pretended to examine a costume for rips.

"Want to celebrate the same way we did last night?"

She turned her back to him and said, "No," in a chilly voice.

He rested one hand against her back, and she sidled away.

"What's wrong? It went fine. I did okay. They were happy."

"Oh, yes," she said. "You did just fine. You acted just fine. You wrote just fine. You did just dandy—all by yourself."

"Hey," he said gently, "it was just a play!"

"It was just a play, but it started out as *my* play. You made it into *your* play. You wrote it. You made fun of me."

"Lisa. Be sensible. It was all farce. Everybody had a wonderful time. Most of them will be coming back for the other plays."

"I don't care," she said. "You had no business to . . . to . . . to ruin my play," she managed to gulp. *And to enjoy doing it so much.* Kissing Helene as if he were Rhett Butler and Helene, Scarlett O'Hara.

In another moment, she'd be crying visible tears, splashing them over the costumes in her arms.

She shrugged off his hands, and, gathering up the rest of the costumes, dashed to her room.

Lisa started the Sunday performance, then went back to her office where she sat in front of the laptop for forty-five minutes. Maybe if she went back to the old ways— She pushed the computer aside, and stared at blank paper, and chewed the end of a ballpoint pen. The excuse she gave herself for ducking out was the Christmas show, but the truth was, she couldn't stand to watch Clinton and Helene mutilating her play.

It was *her* play, the first really important creative thing she'd ever done. It was like a baby. It was the same as Clinton dressing her baby in a clown costume and taking it out in the streets for people to make fun of. How could he?

On top of all that, they hadn't even given her credit for the idea.

She forced her mind back to the Christmas show.

Ideas wouldn't come. She found herself doodling on the paper instead, and then writing the same words over and over. She idly read what she'd traced, and, startled, saw the words *In such a night as this. . . .*

She completely forgot the passage of time until she heard a tap on her door.

"Yes," she called, but Clinton had already let himself in.

"Lisa," he said, "snap out of it. Why weren't you at the performance? Why aren't you out there right now in your hostess-of-the-year role, telling everybody how nice it was that they could come, and that they must be sure to come back every month thereafter?''

She gasped. ''Oh,'' she said. ''Yes, I did need to do that. I forgot. I got so immersed in the Christmas script. That's what I was doing. I was doing the Christmas script. I'll go right out!''

''It's too late,'' he said. ''I already did it, although not, perhaps, with the same flair.''

He moved around the desk, stroking her back, pulling her against him. He read aloud, '' 'In such a night as this. . . .' '' and picked up the piece of paper.

She snatched it away and turned it over on the desk.

Clinton finally cornered Lisa on Monday evening. She glowered at him as he lit the fire in the lobby fireplace, and brought her to sit in the big chair beside it, parking himself on the floor at her feet. He'd come armed with a clipboard, several sheets of paper, and two pens. He handed her the clipboard and one of the pens.

''Now, about this Christmas show, Lisa,'' he said. ''I don't think you've done much on it. Want to bounce some ideas off me?''

''Why don't you just write the play, Clinton? You seem to be much better at it than I am.''

She kicked off her shoes, and pulled her feet up under her in the chair, carefully avoiding any contact with Clinton. If she was going to concentrate on this Christmas play, she mustn't touch him. Unless she watched herself very vigilantly, touching him was the only thing she ever thought about.

''Look,'' he said. ''I'm sorry. Okay. I didn't know you'd mind. And I couldn't change it back for yesterday without explaining to Helene and making a big deal of it. Now let's get on with the next one. What do you have so far?''

Yes. She had been unfair. She knew that. The pressure of getting ready for this weekend, the knowledge of how important it was to the inn, the almost-failure of the first night, and the panic of worrying about the second—yes, all these things had made her far too fast to take offense.

Worst of all—how could she possibly have felt even a little bit jealous of poor Helene?

''Well,'' she said, more cheerfully, ''it's going to have to be about Christmas.''

''Obviously. That's why we keep referring to it as the Christmas show. And I suppose it's going to be about love, because that's why we keep advertising it as a romance weekend.''

She took a deep breath. ''I've been thinking,'' she said. ''Why don't we advertise those four weeks as family weekend month? I thought maybe we could provide a baby-sitting service. That way, people could come for the weekend, and on Saturday leave their kids with us, while they go, unencumbered, Christmas shopping in Halifax or Bridgewater. Then they'll come back in time for dinner, and, of course, for the evening show.''

''Ahem. It does sound like a seller. Even without the show.''

''So that means a kid-centered play,'' Lisa said. ''Lots of extras' parts for children. Believe it or not, I have been thinking about it, even if I didn't get anything down on paper. What about something set in Santa's workshop? All those kids could be elves.''

''Problem. Who's going to have the romance? Santa and his wife? They're getting a bit long in the tooth.''

She sighed. ''I know.''

She went on, "Maybe a family of kids whose dad is a widower and they find him a wife."

"Nah—that's too serious."

"Well, what about this?" she asked, as a sudden inspiration struck. "What about a family of street kids, you know, orphans, runaways, kids from broken homes, whatever, really *nice* street kids.

"Anyway, these street kids decide that, just for Christmas, they want a real family, complete with mother and father, and turkey, and gifts. So these street kids kidnap two people, a man and a woman, and hold them in this old house."

She rushed on, uninhibited now that the ideas were coming. "Well, anyway," she concluded, "the two people they've kidnapped fall in love and get married and adopt all the street kids, just in time for Christmas. Right?"

"Hmm," he said. "Yes, it might be a winner. Work on it. Can you can keep it light and funny?"

"I think so. And then, we'll have carolers, and that will give us more extras. And I'll get together some tapes of the carols, so that everybody will sing along. If they get to singing Christmas carols at the end, they'll forget any little imperfections in the show.

"And they'll have such a good time that they'll come back again and again this season, and then next season, and—"

She read his face and stopped cold. She'd been running on again, the eternal optimist, forgetting that the inn might close, that there might never be another season, that there might not be much more of this season.

"Oh, Clinton," she said, forgetting her own resentment over the play. She slipped down off her chair, beside him on the floor, and wound both arms about his neck.

"Lisa." He reached for her, then drew back. "We mustn't," he said.

"It's all right," she whispered, as she drew one hand across the plane of his cheek. "This is the lobby, and we still have the caretaker and the housekeeper on duty. You can't possibly attack me here." She added, "And I can't attack you either."

His answer was to search for her mouth with his. Here like this, holding Lisa, kissing Lisa, he felt as if he could take on all the Jennifers and country inns in the world and come out on top.

"Oh, Lisa, Lisa," he murmured, "I—"

He stopped. "No," he murmured. "Not until . . ."

Chapter Nine

The next three weekends flew by. Helene attended faithfully. Through her, Lisa discovered a drama student who was willing as well as older and more responsible than the departed Adam.

Attendance grew steadily—except for the weekend that Jennifer flew down, which happened to coincide with Halloween, Halifax's version of Mardi Gras, a professional hockey game in Halifax, and Neptune Theatre's most popular play of the season.

Weekdays, Lisa put in long hours writing the Christmas romance. When she'd thought it out and summarized it she sat Clinton down in front of the fire and showed him the outline about four street waifs who kidnapped parents for a real family Christmas.

"You like?" she asked.

"Yes, Elizabeth Louise, I like."

"You liked the other one, too," she said. "But you still couldn't resist tinkering with it when you got the chance."

"Look, Lisa," he said. "I'm sorry. I told you that. I had no idea you were going to get so bent out of shape over another layer of farce on top all the existing farce." He held up one hand like a Boy Scout taking an oath. "I will resist any temptation to tinker with your little play. Forgiven?"

This time the words "little play" acted like a percussion cap. Lisa exploded. "No," she said. "No, you're not. That's just what I was talking about. Don't you see? You don't value me as a professional woman. I'm just good old Lisa, general handyperson. I take care of the mail. I type. I sew. I do bookkeeping. If the inn didn't have a dining room, I'd make your coffee. If I have spare time and want to toss off a few "little plays," that's okay too.

"Don't you understand? You're a male chauvinist. You do important things, and I do the things you don't want to do. The things that are beneath you. The things that aren't man-stuff.

"Oh, yes, and you kiss me. You've made it very clear from the very beginning, however, that your kisses don't mean anything. They don't value me as a person. I'm just a warm pair of lips. You like kissing, and if I happen to enjoy it too, well that's fine, but I mustn't get above my station to the degree of thinking you mean anything by it. You don't consider me as an equal partner. In kissing or in anything else!"

Clinton looked at her, stunned and astonished, as if his favorite teddy bear had just sprouted quills, fangs, and horns.

"Don't you understand what I'm saying?" she asked

earnestly, no longer fuming, just wanting him to understand. "I've been rereading *A Doll's House*, and that says
it all. Torvald refuses to think of Nora as anything but an
empty-headed little possession, and when she complains
that isn't good enough, he's dumbfounded, and reminds her
she's first and foremost a wife and mother, that is, his prop-
erty. She tells him, 'I don't believe that anymore. I believe
that before all else I am a human being, just as you are.'
All she wanted was to be taken seriously. And that's it
exactly. Don't you understand?''

"I'm not sure," he said. "I know you're a lot more to
me than a warm pair of lips. As for the rest, I guess I'll
have to think about it."

Under his breath, he muttered, "Maybe I'd better reread
my Ibsen."

The weekends of the Christmas show went just as they
were supposed to. Lisa tracked down two theater students
who entered into their parts with verve and enthusiasm. The
baby-sitting feature was a roaring success: for the parents,
freed for Christmas shopping; for the children, who loved
the atmosphere of the inn; for the high-school girls, who
earned extra spending money for Christmas.

"There's only one problem," Lisa said to Clinton as
they sat before the fire.

"What's that?"

"Our two students can't stay for the final weekend. It's
too close to Christmas and exams. They told me from the
beginning, but they're all I had, and I hoped I could find
somebody else for that performance, maybe even a couple
of talented guests. But it hasn't worked."

"Nobody?"

"Absolutely nobody."

"Not even Helene?"

"Not even Helene. Believe it or not, I got so desperate I phoned her and pleaded and groveled, even though she would be totally inappropriate for Louise, but she's off to visit relatives in Vancouver until after Christmas. All the university students have exams, and right before Christmas the bored housewives that used to be aspiring actresses are too busy to be bored. As the saying goes, 'It's you and me, kid.' "

"What do you mean?"

"Just what I said. You, Alex; me, Louise. You wanted a heroine with dimples and brown eyes. You've got her."

"Lisa," he protested, "you can't mean this. After the last time, didn't you promise you'd never, ever, ask me again."

"Clinton, tell me. Is the inn, or isn't the inn, making money?"

"Yes," he admitted. "The inn is making money."

"And isn't this the off-season, where hoping to break even was the best possible scenario?"

"Yes, Lisa. This is the off-season, where hoping to break even was the best possible scenario. In fact, hoping to break even was beyond my wildest dreams."

"And don't you want the inn to continue to make money? Don't you want to surprise your Aunt Jennifer with a balance sheet that has black numbers written all over it? Don't you want to make Jennifer admit the inn is a winner—all year around?"

"Yes. Yes, I do. Yes, and yes, and yes. But isn't there any other way?"

"No," she said. "There isn't any other way."

He tried to put an arm around her.

She drew away. "You're still thinking about it, Clinton. Remember?"

"Lisa," he said, "please, darling. We're not characters in a play. We're us. Lisa, I love you. I want you. I want to marry you, but first I have to get a position that leaves me in the same place more than a few months at a time. And that could take years. It's not fair to you to push you into a formal engagement, to expect you to wait."

"Clinton," she said, placing her hand on his arm, "don't you see? That's exactly what I'm talking about. You say you want to marry me, but you're making all the decisions about when this will happen. If I loved you, and if I wanted to marry you, don't you think I should have some choice about whether I want to wait or whether I want to work beside you to build our future, as partners? Not that I necessarily want to marry you, of course."

Clinton gazed at her, not mocking, not teasing, but out of tired, strained eyes. She blinked back tears at seeing his dear face looking that way. Because of her.

"Well, I want to marry you, Lisa," he said, his voice hoarse. "It's all I've thought about since I met you. I love you and I want to marry you, but right now I can't. When I tease you, and make fun of you, and even when I kiss you and then stop, it's because I can't bear not being able to have you, and I'm protecting myself as best I can."

"Oh, Clinton. I'm sorry," she said. "I've no right to play silly little female games. Of course, I love you. You know that. And if we love each other, I don't see why we can't do something about it—now.

"Now! I mean it, Clinton Daniels! I love you and you say you love me. Now, you either do something about it, right now, or go back to being my employer. I can't stand this. You just set a wedding date—now—for yesterday if not sooner, and, until you do, I'm nothing but your recreation director and secretary. That's it. Either your employee, or your wife and equal. Nothing in between.'' She crisscrossed her hands in a rapid emphatic gesture to underline her words.

"Lisa, please. Don't you understand? I love you too much to expect you to settle for this.''

"Settle for what? You haven't even told me that yet, have you? The unemployed English professor who drives a beat-up old station wagon and can't get married because he can't afford a house? The morning after that first disaster, Jennifer and I talked about more than grapefruit games.''

"Oh.''

"Yes. Oh. We discussed things like Jaguars. And salaries. Things you never saw fit to tell me, regardless of how much you love me. Anything further you'd like to share?''

"All right. Yes. You're angry about that, and I can't blame you. I didn't tell you at first, because at first you were an employee, the same as the others. After I realized I loved you, I didn't know how to admit I'd been lying— or at least telling you only partial truths. Remember the quotation that says something like, 'What tangled webs we mortals weave when first we practice to deceive'? Don't you understand?''

She sighed. "Yes,'' she said. "I guess I do. But it was still a shock to find out from Jennifer.''

"It doesn't make marriage any easier,'' he said. "Sure, I can afford it. But my job has me running all over North America and a few places out of it. That's no family life. And this time, I am telling the truth. The whole truth.''

"I hope so. Your choice, Clinton,'' she added as she scrambled to her feet. "Make up your mind.''

The final show opened with Clinton and Lisa tied up, sitting back to back.

"What's going on here?" he said to her, in character.

She replied, "I don't know. I think they're all kids."

In the next scene, they all sat around a kitchen table, the kids telling Alex and Louise how they tried to take care of one another, but how they wanted real parents for Christmas. The room became very quiet.

Lisa saw handkerchiefs coming out and women wiping their eyes. This had also happened at the earlier performances. She rejoiced that every performance had been a winner—a real one, not just one which was funny because it was so bad.

At the end, when they told the children they would get married and adopt them and they would all live together, there wasn't a dry eye in the house.

Alex enveloped everybody in a hug before he moved to Louise, took her in his arms, and kissed her, just as enthusiastically as he'd kissed Helene in *The Gypsies of Mahone Bay*, but somewhere in the middle of the kiss, instead of Alex kissing Louise, Clinton was kissing Lisa. The children stepped aside and clapped and cheered along with everybody else.

Lisa sat in her room when the play was over. It was like Friday night when she'd been teaching—the time of suspension between one thing and another.

The guests had left. The only sounds were the roars of the big trucks on the highway, bearing loads of Christmas trees to Boston and New York.

Lisa opened the drapes and gazed at the full moon over the gravel parking lot. There'd been a moon like that the night she sat with Clinton on the front steps and parodied quotations from *The Merchant of Venice*. This would not be a night to sit outside. There was still no snow, but earlier in the week there'd been freezing rain, and, since then, sharp frosts each night. The weather had stayed clear and cold.

Except for the kisses during the play, the closeness with Clinton had ended when she'd demanded that if he loved her he'd better do something about it. Her heart was breaking, but she wasn't sorry about what she'd said. She couldn't bear the constant pursuing, the drawing back, and, now, the insistence he loved her but couldn't marry her until some mythical time when he had some type of job that kept him home more.

What she had told him was true.

It was time for him to make up his mind. If he loved her as he said, he must ask her to marry him now, and assure her she would be an equal partner in the marriage. If he didn't have that much faith in their future together, he should treat her as a valued professional colleague and employee.

There was a rap on her door. She sighed. Clinton. What now? She resolved there'd be no repetition of the emotional seesaw he always put her on.

She opened the door. Clinton stood there dressed in jeans and a heavy outdoor sweater and mittens, a pair of ice skates over his shoulder, a portable sound system and a flashlight swinging from one hand.

''Come on, Lisa,'' he said. ''Put on a warm sweater and socks and bring your skates. The pond's frozen.''

He closed the door to wait in her office. Lisa scrambled for suitable clothes, choosing white leggings, with heavy woolen socks drawn over them, a sweatshirt, and, over that, a heavy white fisherman-knit sweater. She knelt on the floor to rummage into the back of the closet where the skates had been thrown amongst other things she rarely used. Then she put on boots and white Angora mittens and a matching headband. She stepped out into the office to join Clinton.

The moon made everything as bright as day. They followed the trail that wound between the shrubs and trees until it ended at the pond.

Lisa caught her breath at the vision spread out before them. The night was still. The film of ice on the pond shone as clear and dark as glass, reflecting the moon in a path of light which transversed it. Above, a canopy of stars twinkled in the frosty night. Late though it was, the sky itself seemed a deep indigo blue rather than the black of night.

"Here," Clinton said, shining the flashlight onto a fallen log at the edge of the pond. "Just sit here."

She sat down, and started unlacing her boots.

"No," he said. "Let me."

He pulled off his mittens and knelt on the frozen ground.

Lisa watched his strong fingers and capable hands as he untied and loosened the laces of her winter boots. He drew the boots off gently, running his hands over the woolen socks, smoothing away each lump and easing on the white figure skates, lacing up each one, tightening the laces as he went.

"There you go," he said.

It was what he'd said the first day when he'd carried her belongings from the car.

He helped her to her feet. She picked her way across the frozen ground as dainty and careful as a cat through mud. When she reached the ice, she bent down swiftly, removed the skate guards, and handed them to him. When he released her hand, she spun away, gliding without effort over the sheen of ice.

He sat down and watched, making no effort to put on his own skates.

Lisa felt free and whole. It was like being released from a dusty cell. The whole summer and fall had gone in a haze of work, of typing, of sewing, of writing. She'd gone outdoors only to clear trails or take kids for hikes.

She skated in wide circles, drawing white lines that marred the clear surface of the lake. Her muscles stretched and responded. She went into some of her more acrobatic figure-skating routines: twirling, spinning, leaping into the air. She skated back to Clinton's side of the lake.

Using her mittened hands as a megaphone, she yelled into them, cheerleader fashion. "Give me an L." No response. "Come on, Clinton. Give me an L."

"L," he said.

"Give me a U."

The response was louder this time.

"Give me an N."

"N," Clinton shouted back.

She danced on her skates, back and forth, raising her knees, marching on the spot, swinging her shoulders and clapping her hands.

The cheer went on.

As she ended, "Lunenburg Whaler, rah, rah, rah!" she leaped into the air, both feet tucked under her; as she came down, she slipped gracefully onto the ice in the splits.

A second later, she was off again, circling the pond in dizzying circles, leaping into the air and landing on her skates.

Clinton watched, hypnotized.

What had he done? He'd caged a jeweled hummingbird and treated it like a plain brown wren. He'd harnessed silver-winged Pegasus to a plow. He'd captured Titania and chained her in front of a computer and a sewing machine.

He watched a Lisa he'd never seen before. She flashed before him, white in the moonlight, silhouetted against the dark sky and the dark ice, along with the tracery of winter birch. The ice-coated branches of winter trees and glazed cattails at the edge of the pond shimmered in the moonlight like a billion diamonds, joining the moon and the twinkling stars in setting off the glory that was Lisa.

She was dressed all in white: the headband, the bulky sweater, the white mittens, the leggings and the skates, a blurring flash of innocent white. She was an angel against the backdrop of eternity; she was a fairy queen surrounded by the night; she was Aurora caught out after dark; she was Iris silhouetted against a purple sky.

She bounded like a deer, she twirled like a genie escaping from his bottle, she glided like a downy feather in a gentle breeze. She stopped and waved at Clinton, beckoning him to come out, to join her.

He could have sat on the log forever, watching as her gracefulness flowed into the night. But her waving arm called to him. He exchanged his winter boots for hockey skates, feeling like a yokel heading out clumsily onto the farm dugout when he compared himself and his old skates to the glancing brilliance of Lisa in motion.

After he removed his skate guards, he pushed the play button on the tape recorder, sending the notes of the ''Skater's Waltz'' into the night air. Lisa's skating slowed and gentled to match the rhythm of the music as she glided up to him and took his hand. The two of them circled the lake.

She moved her hands to take his left in her left, his right in her right, crossing their hands in front of them, as skating couples do. They skated with long rhythmic strokes. Then she shook her hands against his and said, "Now." On that signal, they reversed directions and skated around again.

The selection came to an end, and, after a pause, the haunting melody of "The Blue Skirt Waltz" filled the night air. Lisa shifted her position to face him, her hands linked behind his neck. He placed his hands gingerly, almost reverently, on either side of her waist.

She sang with the music, looking up into his face, her brown eyes huge and black in the moonlight.

He had an ache in his throat looking down on her. Her voice rang clear and true. Yes, he'd heard her sing before. She'd led the guests in carol singing at the end of the Christmas romance. He'd never heard her voice by itself as it was now, rising into the clear and frosty air.

He looked down into her eyes, silent. He couldn't sing like she could; it seemed sacrilege to even try to join her. No teasing comments hovered on his lips. He could only skate in time with the music, in harmony with her.

And she loved him. The thought of it seemed a miracle. She was an angel and she loved him. She trembled when she was in his arms. She quivered when he kissed her. All she demanded was that he see her as a person equal to himself.

He'd wanted to protect her, to care for her. He still did—tonight more than ever. He'd wanted to put off the final commitment until he was sure of what he could offer her. But she, like Ibsen's Nora Helmer, insisted on working with him, beside him, to be his equal partner through good times and bad.

This piece of gossamer floating between his hands, seemingly as fragile and delicate as morning dew, moving in perfect harmony with him, was really spun of the finest, strongest steel. She wanted him to recognize that, not in exploitation but in an equal partnership.

The tape ended. They skated back to shore. Clinton removed her skates and then his own. He slung his skates over his shoulder, picked up the sound system and the flashlight in one hand, and reached out for her hand with the other.

Wordlessly she took the flashlight from him, then put her free hand in his. They walked back in silence through the night.

At her door, she lifted her face for his good-night kiss.

He dropped his skates and the sound system onto the floor, tugged one mitten off with his teeth, then removed the other. He took her skates from over her shoulder and the flashlight from her hand, adding them to the growing pile of objects on the floor.

"Don't move." With his hands, he reached out to frame her face.

She gazed at him, mute, under the dim lighting in the hallway. His fingers stroked her cheek with reverence.

Lisa sensed something flowing between them, from Clinton's fingers to her face and back again. It wasn't the electric flash of longing she'd felt so often when he touched her: it was something bigger and deeper, an enduring life force rather than an exploding flame, the constant cadence of eternal tides rather than the evanescent flicker of heat lightning.

With one finger, he circled and caressed the contours of her ear. In that gesture, it seemed to Lisa that their very souls touched, her soul being drawn into him through the whisper of his fingers against her skin, his soul entering into her.

He dropped his hands with a final stroking caress. She looked into his face intently. There was no laughter, no teasing there. She couldn't speak.

"Good night, Lisa," he whispered. "I've got a lot of heavy thinking to do. Try to trust me, darling."

She watched as he picked up his belongings and retreated down the hall; then she picked up her own and went into her room.

Something had happened tonight. She couldn't put it into words, but somehow her relationship with Clinton had moved on, past mere attraction and infatuation. He hadn't so much as kissed her good night, but in those subtle touches against her cheeks and ear, there'd been more love expressed than in their most passionate clinches.

Her heart was not racing, nor her pulse pounding, but a deep contentment bathed every cell and every pore in her body.

"Try to trust me, darling," he had said.

Clinton knew Lisa was right. He must accept her terms, when he had been so fortunate as to have her love him, to have had her keep loving him through his inconsistency and indecision.

In these past few days, he'd made up his mind. He didn't want to be a business executive. He didn't want to be leaner and meaner. He wanted to stay here at the inn, marry Lisa, do a good job of running his own business and of providing for his own family and his own employees. If all Lisa demanded from him was the right to help him do those things, how could he resist?

But first, he must play a lone hand one more time.

Chapter Ten

Lisa slept well and slept late, with none of the tossing and turning and reliving of kisses that normally followed an evening with Clinton.

She felt wonderful. The pressures of the past six months were behind her. She'd faced challenges unrelated to the many things she'd already known how to do, and she'd coped. She'd been a waitress for the first and only time of her life, under difficult circumstances; she'd become a successful social and recreation director; she'd gone out on a limb with the romance weekends, and had triumphed, both artistically and financially.

Last night had been the "happily ever after" to a fairy tale. She must skate on the pond again, more often. It would not be the same. Last night had been one of those magic moments, to be experienced only once in a lifetime, the same as the night she and Clinton had sat on the steps and quoted Shakespeare at each other.

163

In such a night as this— That night would never come again. Last night would never come again. But that was cause for celebration, not for regret. Each moment was like a precious jewel, to be taken out of its safety deposit box of memory, to be treasured and caressed at intervals, but not to be cloned—no, never to be cloned, never to be hoarded to the exclusion of all the new precious moments of experience.

There would be many of those. Something new had flowed between Clinton and herself last night—something that superseded the teasings and desires of their previous relationship, precious though those were. She and Clinton would marry, and there would be many other magic moments to cherish: his placing his diamond on her finger; their wedding day; their wedding night; the moment she held their first child in her arms and then handed the child to him.

There would be room in life for all of it: for teasing and playing; for petty quarrels; for desire and the satisfying of desire; for exalted moments like last night; for serious responsibilities they would face together.

Lisa sighed. It was time to stop dreaming and get on with the day. She still had the routine work to do.

The mail waited in her office.

She sorted the letters into those she could handle herself and those requiring Clinton's attention first.

There was one from the head office in Toronto, from Jennifer. Aha! Probably congratulating them on the fine job the inn was doing.

Dear Clinton, Lisa read.

This is just to verify what we discussed on the phone the other day. Yes, I am pleased with what you have

*done with the inn over the last two months, but I'm
still afraid that I must close you down at Christmas.*

*As I suggested, you should ask Joe and Maria to
take your apartment for the winter. They will keep an
eye on things in exchange for free rent. . . .*

The letter went on, discussing the mechanics of moth-
balling the inn for the winter, and telling Clinton that Jennifer needed him in the head office for a few months while
she joined Silas in Japan helping him get the new Tokyo
inn in operation. The part Lisa found most humiliating was
the first sentence, the one indicating that Jennifer had already discussed this with Clinton by phone.

He'd known during the final performance. He'd known
when he'd taken her skating. He'd known when he had
whispered to her in the hallway, *"Try to trust me, darling."*

How could she trust him when he didn't ever tell her
anything? It didn't mean he didn't love her. She knew that
now. It meant he still looked down on her, belittling her,
protecting her. She was still Nora Helmer, puttering about
in her little doll's house, being shielded by her big strong
man from all the realities of the wide wicked world out
there.

Where was the partnership she'd wanted from him? Demanded from him? She thought that after last night he'd
looked at her in a different way. Not! She'd been his dancing doll in the moonlight, and he'd been temporarily dis-
tracted by a transcendent feeling for her. That's all. The
feeling certainly was not one of equality.

She began to crumple the letter in her anger, then
stopped, and smoothed it out again, pressing her palm

against each wrinkle. She would take the letter to show him; she would have it out with Clinton Daniels. Now!

She stomped down the hall, letter in hand, and rapped on Clinton's office door; when there was no answer she stormed inside and pounded on his apartment door. Still no answer.

She checked the parking lot. There were only two cars, Joe's and Pink Sally.

Clinton had probably gone into Bridgewater to buy padlocks for all the fire exits before he mothballed the inn. She'd ask Joe.

Joe was sweeping out the remnants of last night's play from the dining room.

"Do you know where Clinton went?"

Joe leaned on his broom handle. "Yes," he said. "To the airport. He left for Toronto early this morning."

"Oh." She was left speechless. "He didn't say anything to me."

Joe shrugged. "Probably didn't want to wake you up. He'll be back in a few days. He said he'd be spending Christmas here, him and Mrs. Masters too."

"Oh. Thanks, Joe." She turned and left.

Didn't want to wake her up! He'd have known about Jennifer's plans last night, if not for two or three days before that. He didn't leave in response to the letter—it hadn't arrived yet. He'd left in response to Jennifer's phone call, if, indeed, it hadn't been a preplanned trip rather than being in response to anything. Busy learning the duties of the head office, no doubt.

That's what he'd wanted all along, wasn't it? To get out of the boondocks and back to Toronto. Bully for Clinton. *"Try to trust me, darling,"* indeed.

She dragged her suitcases from the closet and packed all

the clothes she might need at home for an extended Christmas vacation. When she reached for the ice skates, she felt tears gather on her lashes, then brushed them away.

"Try to trust me, darling."

Getting home didn't help. A letter from Jennifer waited there. Maybe it was a job offer in a different inn. Dartmouth would be fine, but there was no way she'd run after Clinton to Toronto, especially when he hadn't asked her.

She sat at her desk in her cozy pink-and-white room, and slit the envelope with a fingernail. She drew out the letter, pausing a moment, as if by so doing she could ward off whatever evil it might contain.

Finally she unfolded it and spread it out on the surface of her desk.

Dear Lisa,

This is to give you formal notice that the inn will not reopen after Christmas, and that, therefore, your services will no longer be required.

Clinton and I both appreciate your enthusiasm, as well as the fine job you did on all of the various duties you were assigned. This layoff in no way reflects on your work. You may feel free to use my name as a reference if you wish to apply for jobs.

Enclosed please find the forms which will expedite your application for unemployment insurance. We will give you at least one month's notice if we anticipate your position at the inn being available in the spring.

On a happier note, Clinton and I intend to spend Christmas at the inn before we close it up. Silas will be in Japan working on arrangements for the new Tokyo country inn we hope to open in the coming year.

*We would be delighted if you and your parents
would spend Christmas with us. You might like to
come down the day before to visit and help decorate
the tree. Your parents could join us the next day for
Christmas dinner.*

*I do hope you will be able to join us. With best
wishes for your future.*

Jennifer Masters.''

Lisa's hand shook. She took several deep breaths and
read the letter the second time to be sure she hadn't been
dreaming on the first reading.

She hadn't been dreaming. This was what the letter really
and truly said. Mind you, she already knew if the inn were
to close she'd be laid off for the winter. Clinton had told
her that at the interview.

But to be dismissed so coldly, with not a word except
the invitation for Christmas to suggest she was anything
more than just another employee to them.

Had Clinton known about this letter? Was this offhand
dismissal his as well as Jennifer's? Not necessarily. The
letter had been written and posted before Clinton arrived
in Toronto. But Jennifer wrote as if she were writing for
them both, and she must have had some idea of what Clinton
and Lisa meant to each other. Correction. Of what Lisa
had thought she and Clinton meant to each other.

Lisa furiously crumpled the letter into a little ball and
trashed it like the garbage it was.

Her mother's voice carried up the stairs. "Lisa—time
for lunch."

"Coming, Mom." She washed her face and went
downstairs.

When they were seated at the kitchen table over cheese

and bacon sandwiches, Lisa said casually, ''I got a letter from Jennifer. The inn might close for the winter. And she invited us to go down to the inn for Christmas. All of us.'' She added quickly, ''I'm sure you don't want to do that though. We've always had Christmas at home—just you and me and Daddy.''

She couldn't spend Christmas with Clinton, making polite chitchat, asking about his job in Toronto. She'd have to get the rest of her things and have it out with him, but she'd do that the day before or the day after.

''Why not?'' Beth said. ''I think it would be nice to have Christmas dinner for once without cooking it. I've already got my fruitcake made, so I'll take that with me. Your boss seemed a fine young man.'' Lisa's parents had been down twice—once for each play—and had met Clinton on those occasions. ''And you've told us so much about Jennifer Masters. We'd love to meet her.''

Oh, my, thought Lisa. *What do I do now?*

She stooped and kissed her mother's hair as she moved to take her lunch dishes to the sink.

''We'll talk about it later, Mom,'' she said.

''Here,'' Beth said, as she came into the house laden with parcels, ''could you take these things while I get off my boots?''

Lisa was wrapping gifts on the kitchen table. She took the parcels and the newspaper from her mother and placed them on a kitchen chair.

Beth put away her coat and boots and returned wearing house slippers and jeans.

She blew on her hands. ''Whew, it's cold,'' she said. ''I'd love a cup of coffee.''

Lisa said, ''I'll make it. You sit down.''

She moved the wrapping project to one end of the table. Beth sank into a chair, blew on her fingers again, and opened the paper while she waited. She had the habit of going through the newspaper backward, giving a quick glance first at the names of the births, marriages, and obituaries, then moving to the classifieds.

"Oh," she said. "You didn't say anything about the inn being for sale."

Lisa quit breathing.

"Inn?"

"Your inn. The Lunenburg Whaler. You told me it might close for the winter, but you didn't say anything about its being sold."

Lisa was grateful to be busy with the percolator, the water, the coffee, grateful for a moment to keep her back turned. Once she'd plugged in the coffee, she procrastinated further by getting out the mugs, by arranging a few pieces of shortbread in neat rows on a plate, by folding two paper napkins.

"Oh, for heaven's sake, quit fussing," Beth said. "I just want some coffee to warm up. We're not having the queen for tea."

Lisa stood in front of the coffeepot waiting for the red light to come on. Finally it did. She couldn't hide any longer. She poured the coffee into the two mugs, and set them on the table, along with the shortbread and the napkins, then sat down.

"Now then," she said lightly, "could I see that paper?"

She buried her face in her mug while she waited for her mother to flip to the offending page, and fold it back.

"Here," Beth said.

It was a large ad. *For sale, on the picturesque South Shore of Nova Scotia, a flourishing country inn, The Lu-*

nenburg Whaler. The ad went on to give the size, the operating profit in the first season—an amount that seemed astronomical to Lisa—and the asking price.

"Hmm," Beth said. "If it's that profitable I wonder why it's for sale."

"I'm sure I wouldn't know," Lisa said. She got a searching look from her mother.

Lisa avoided Beth's eyes by taking a quick swallow, then choked on her coffee, and went into a spasm of coughing.

"What's the matter? Are you all right?"

Lisa finished coughing and wiped her eyes. "It's all right," she said. "I just swallowed wrong. I'm fine. Really, I am."

It was just as well. Her mother would think she was red-faced and runny-eyed because of the coughing spell.

Lisa put her mug down with a thump. "Excuse me," she said, "I'd better hide these before Daddy gets home." She grabbed two of the wrapped presents and fled to the cozy room with the pink carpet and the rose-covered wallpaper.

She sat on the bed, biting her lip to keep back the tears. He wasn't worth crying over, she told herself. Her first impression of him had been the right one.

He was nothing but a wolf. They'd cuddled and they'd kissed, and he'd even said, "I love you." And he had said, "I'd like to marry you, but—"

"I love you" was an easy thing to say. The standard line. When she stopped to think about it, they'd never had a real date.

What had they had? A lot of close companionship in the workplace, and a lot of kissing and hugging. She'd taken too much for granted because of that, and finally because he'd said, "I love you." She should have known better.

She'd done a lot of dating in her life and many of the partners had said "I love you." She'd chalked up their enthusiasm to the soft lips and the balmy nights and had said things like, "I love you, too, as a dear, dear friend. Let's not spoil the beautiful times we've shared."

Clinton was just a wolf. He'd had a little fun with stupid Lisa with her enthusiasms about grapefruit games and romance weekends. He'd kissed her a few times and finally kept her quiet by going to the old "I love you and I'd really like to marry you" line, and had likely had a good laugh when she swallowed it.

He probably told his rich friends in Toronto all the funny little Lisa stories and laughed with them over the unqualified recreation director and all her faux pas.

He didn't love her. Love was a partnership. Love wasn't lacking the guts to tell her the inn was closing down for the winter. Love wasn't letting her find out in the newspaper that the inn she'd helped put together from the ground up was being sold. Love wasn't letting her think he was an unemployed professor with a beat-up old station wagon.

For one wild moment she began to think of excuses for avoiding Christmas, for convincing her mother, even at this point, but she remembered, *That's not performance.*

She had to face it. No matter how much it hurt, she would go to the inn. She would smile, not warmly it was true, at Clinton and Jennifer. She would help trim the tree, and she would thank Clinton for the box of chocolates he would probably get her for Christmas.

Until she got him alone—away from Jennifer—away from her parents—and then she would let him know what she thought of a friend who would treat a friend so shabbily.

She would not kiss him anymore. Certainly not. No matter how much he smiled and dimpled his dimples and teased and ran his fingers around her ear.

She washed her face, took some unwrapped gifts out of the closet, and marched downstairs.

It was mid-afternoon when Lisa turned into the driveway of the inn. Jennifer's rental car was in the parking lot, along with Clinton's wagon.

By time Lisa had her bags lifted from the trunk Clinton was at her side.

He enveloped her in a bear hug. He looked so satisfied with himself that he was almost smirking.

She reminded herself to behave pleasantly and turned a cool cheek to be kissed.

"It's wonderful to have you back," Clinton said.

"It's very pleasant to be here," Lisa said stiffly.

"What the—" Clinton said, then shrugged and picked up her suitcase.

Now was as good a time as any.

"You look very pleased with yourself this morning, Clinton. I suppose you've successfully sold the inn, and now you're happily out of the boondocks, heading for the big city."

"Oh," he said. "How did you know the inn was for sale?"

"I read it in the paper. I'm sure it would be a frosty Friday before I heard it from you." She repeated, "And you're looking so pleased with yourself this morning that I suppose you've sold it."

He gave her a searching look, pretending to be serious, the dimple in his left cheek giving him away. "Lisa," he said, "I didn't know when I left for Toronto that the inn was to be sold, and that's the truth. But yes, as a matter of fact, Jennifer has sold it.''

"Oooh," Lisa said. "Oooh." The tears she couldn't keep back froze on her lashes.

"It's all right. You can probably get a job with the new owner. You'll come highly recommended.''

He brushed his hand across her face to wipe away her tears. "Sorry," he said.

"Listen, sweetheart," he added, "I think we have to talk. It's too cold out here, and Jennifer's in the lobby. Let's head through the back door and into your office.''

She trudged after him over the frozen ground, through the back door, and into her own office—well, into what used to be her own office. He tossed her bags into her room, and helped her off with her coat and boots, then settled her into the easy chair and hunkered down before her.

"Lisa," he said, "listen, sweetheart, I love you.''

"Oh," she said, carefully filtering the sarcasm from her voice, "you mean you're asking me to go Toronto with you?''

"Toronto? What makes you think I'm going to Toronto?''

"That's no mystery. Your letter from Jennifer came just after you left. I read it—like I do all the mail that's not marked PERSONAL. I do the mail, I type the letters, I sew, and wait on tables, and run the recreation programs, and write and produce romances, and I helped this inn to make such a nice profit that it was a major selling point in the ad in the paper.

"But am I important enough to be told things like the inn's closing down, you're going to Toronto, the inn is being sold? Oh, yes, Lisa, I love you, but don't worry your pretty little empty head about any of those things. Just keep typing.''

Sounding like a broken record, Clinton said again, ''Lisa, I love you.''

''And you're asking me to go Toronto. Right?''

He laid his hands on hers. She didn't have enough energy to stop him.

He smiled at her, and the dimples that she loved teased.

''No, Lisa,'' he said. ''I'm not taking you to Toronto.''

''So you love me. But you're not taking me to Toronto. I suppose there's somebody else you love in Toronto. And do you love a woman everywhere that S and J has a country inn? You love Lisa here. And Debbie in Dartmouth and Molly in Montreal, and Cathy in Calgary, I suppose, and one in Winnipeg and one in Edmonton and one in Vancouver. Oooh!

''Just listen to me, Clinton Daniels,'' she continued, ''we are both here for Christmas, and Jennifer is here, and my parents are coming and once I calm down I will act in a civilized fashion and we will spend the next two days behaving as if we were friends. But there will be no more talk of love and there will be no more kissing. Do I make myself quite, quite clear?''

''Oh, quite,'' Clinton said. He didn't seem nearly as contrite as he should.

''Listen, Lisa,'' he said, his face serious, ''just listen a moment. You are not out of a job. I can tell you that much. I've talked to the new owner. You will continue, complete with romance weekends, after Christmas. And so will I. We will both have jobs here. We will still be together. The same as we were before.''

''Oh. Oh. The same as we were before. But that, Clinton Daniels, is not good enough!''

It wasn't good enough. She'd told him the truth about that. This whole thing had to end, one way or the other.

She stood up abruptly, almost knocking him to the floor. "Now, Clinton," she said, "why don't we just prepare to celebrate Christmas?"

When they entered the lobby, Jennifer sat in front of the fireplace smoking. She stubbed out her cigarette and walked across the room to embrace Lisa and give her a friendly kiss.

They drank tea and ate Christmas cookies in front of the fire. After dinner they decorated the big tree that Clinton had brought into the lobby that morning.

It would have been a perfect evening, Lisa thought, if Clinton truly loved her, if they were preparing to marry, if things were as they had seemed that night they skated together on the pond. But she was cool, and Clinton was smug, and Jennifer looked disappointed. It was a horrible evening.

The only redeeming feature was the phone call from Helene wishing them a merry Christmas, and telling them she'd met a retired vacuum-cleaner salesman and wouldn't be coming back to Nova Scotia.

Bully for Helene. Good thing this Christmas was turning out right for somebody.

Christmas day dawned still and snow covered. The trees wore white, and a blanket of snow covered the gravel parking lot.

Lisa looked out her window. It should have been an enchanted world. Light snow still fell, big fluffy flakes, like snowflakes on Christmas cards. When she was a child, her mother had told her that snow like this came from Mother Goose shaking her feather bed.

She wondered how to dress. She might be heartbroken, but she didn't intend to look it. She chose a pair of bright red Chinese lounging pajamas of quilted satin, embroidered across the top with a huge black fire-breathing dragon. What could be more appropriate for a Christmas-card Christmas morning or even for a might-have-been Christmas-card morning! With them, she put on a pair of black slippers shaped like elfin boots. She marched to the dining room.

Jennifer and Clinton sat beside a bubbling coffeepot.

Clinton looked up and whistled.

"You look lovely, my dear," Jennifer said, as she poured coffee for Lisa and kissed her on the cheek. "Now, why don't you sit down here and have your morning coffee with Clinton, while I dish up the eggs Benedict."

They drank coffee in silence for a few moments.

"She was right, you know," Clinton said. "That outfit is gorgeous on you. You are more than lovely—you're beautiful."

She glared at him.

Jennifer came back into the room carrying a tray loaded with homemade muffins and eggs Benedict.

After she had unloaded the tray and sat down, she raised her coffee cup. "To us," she said, "to us, and to the continued success of The Lunenburg Whaler."

Under its new owners, of course, thought Lisa.

When they finished eating, they went into the lobby and seated themselves around the Christmas tree.

The three of them opened their gifts from each other: a gourmet cookbook for Jennifer from Lisa, a ski sweater for Clinton from Lisa, an exquisite beaded Angora sweater for evening wear for Lisa from Jennifer.

There had been presents from everybody to everybody,

except from Clinton to Lisa. Giving him even something as impersonal as the ski sweater was an embarrassment if he wasn't going to give her anything. There were no more presents left under the tree.

Clinton left the room and returned dragging a huge cardboard box, wrapped and beribboned, and punched full of holes.

He placed the box in front of Lisa. Some very peculiar sounds came from it. The tag on it read, *To Elizabeth Louise from Clinton.*

"Go on," Clinton urged. "Open it!"

Lisa shrugged, and gingerly began to undo the ribbons and the Christmas paper that covered the box. The top of the box was folded down, half of each flap tucked over the one beside it. The noises became louder and even more peculiar. The box appeared ready to roll over on its own.

"Go on," Clinton urged. "Open the box!"

Lisa undid the flaps so that they stood upright, only to discover wire mesh. Then she realized! A puppy. In a puppy cage.

Eagerly she tore the box down to where she could lift out the cage, and see the gangling wolfhound puppy within. She opened the cage door, and the pup raced out, all legs and ears and long hair, cavorting around, romping, putting its front paws flat on the floor, so it looked as if it were kneeling. It jumped on Lisa, licking her face, then bounded off and then back again.

She pulled it to her, holding it on her lap, nuzzling her face in its fur, rubbing it the way she knew dogs liked to be rubbed.

"Thank you, Clinton," she said.

"And what are you going to name it?" he asked.

"Nicholas Alexander," she said. "What else? Nicky for short, I suppose."

"Here," Clinton said to Jennifer, "would you take this wretched hound and Elizabeth Louise out of here!"

Jennifer scooped up the dog. Lisa, more than a little miffed, began to get to her feet.

He took her hand, and pulled her back down beside him. "Oh, no," he said and rolled his eyes and dimpled his dimples. "Not you. Just Elizabeth Louise. I want to get Elizabeth Louise and that dog out of the way so I can have my wicked way with Lisa."

Jennifer smiled and padded backward from the room.

"Oh, no," Clinton said again, more softly this time. "Not Lisa. I have more gifts for Lisa."

He handed her a thick envelope. She looked at it, puzzled. "Open it," he said.

She opened it and spread out the documents it contained. The first page had Clinton's name on it, and Lisa's, and there were a lot of things about the party of the first part and the party of the second part.

"I don't understand," she said.

"It's ours, Lisa. It's my surprise for you. It's the agreement of sale for The Lunenburg Whaler. It's not final, of course. Because your name is on it, there are things you'll have to sign."

Lisa's mouth went dry. She licked her lips with the tip of her tongue, and looked at Clinton, bewildered.

"I bought it," he said. "For us. When Jennifer told me she was adamant about closing the inn, I flew to Toronto to talk her out of it. By that time she'd decided to put it up for sale and already had the ad in the paper. The company needed ready cash for the expansion into Japan. So I bought it. I told them that this is what I want—what you and I want. Even if I won't make as much money as I did. We'll reopen after Christmas.''

''You mean,'' Lisa said, ''that we, you and I, own The Lunenburg Whaler, as partners?''

''If you want,'' he said. ''If you're not ready for that much equality, you can still go on working here, for me.''

She sat a moment, stunned. ''Put your money where your mouth is. Is that what you're telling me, Clinton?''

''If that's what you want,'' he said. ''I'm not finished. I'd like us to be partners in more than The Lunenburg Whaler.''

From his pocket, he took out a small package and handed it to her.

She unfastened the ribbon and tore off the paper to find an exquisite velvet box.

She opened it and caught her breath. Inside, nestled in the rich blue velvet case, were a solitaire diamond and a matching wedding band.

She couldn't think of anything to say, so she said, ''How did you know my size?''

''Jennifer. She helped me pick it out. She knew your fingers were the same size as hers. Remember that night of the opening when you put her ring on? She has excellent taste, but if you don't like it, we can exchange it.''

''Oh, Clinton.''

He reached for her and drew her into his arms. ''Will you take them, Lisa? I'm good at teasing and flirting, maybe not so good when it's real. I've had trouble putting how I feel about you into words, so I've teased and plagued. But I do love you, Lisa. I really do. I think I've loved you from the very beginning.

''Not Elizabeth Louise. It's Lisa I love. Sweet and pretty and kind. Marry me. I'm afraid all I have to offer you now is this inn, but we've been a good team. I know I've been a male chauvinist pig, but I'm going to change. I told you that night we skated I had some heavy thinking to do. Well, I did it. I just had to give you the deed to the inn as a Christmas surprise, but that's the last thing. We'll be partners in everything from now on. I promise. If you'll just marry me. Please, Lisa. As soon as we can make arrangements. I know we'll do well. In our marriage and in the inn. We're a good team.''

She smiled at him, tears misting on her eyelashes. ''Oh, Clinton,'' she said. ''Yes, we are a good team, aren't we? I love you too. I think that's why I was willing to do anything to keep the place open this winter. I was so afraid if it closed up and I went home and you went away, I'd never see you again. I couldn't have stood that.'' She sighed. ''I especially couldn't bear the thought of you going to Toronto and finding someone else.''

She held out her left hand for Clinton to slip on the ring, and sat and gazed at it as if bewitched.

Clinton was finally hers, all hers, her very own, to tease and torment her and love her forever and ever, all the rest of her life.

Lisa smiled. Imagine Clinton remembering about Elizabeth Louise and the wolfhounds. She'd keep Nicky. But she didn't need the rest of her long-ago imaginary life, the mink coats and suede suits and limousines and obedient and manageable lovers. She had everything she wanted here: a real job, a real inn, Clinton.

Clinton moved his hand around her face the way she loved, stroking behind her ears, and down her jaw. She took his face between her hands, and explored his dimples with her fingertips. Her heart was so full that the words for it weren't there, so she didn't even try.

Instead, she gave him an impish grin and said, "And you know something? I think I have the plot for the Valentine show. There's this country inn that's barely built. It has an imaginary swimming pool and imaginary tennis courts. If you stand on top of the imaginary second story you have an imaginary view of the coast. The manager is an unemployed English professor and the social director is an unemployed elementary schoolteacher. But somehow, even though they don't have any idea what they're doing, because they work hard and love each other, they—"

"Get married and live happily ever after!" he finished for her, as he gathered her to him, and the kiss he had for her most definitely assured her that he was neither obedient nor manageable. The kiss she had for him assured him most emphatically that his bride-to-be was not the cold beauty of Elizabeth Louise, but the warm and eager reality of Lisa.